P9-BJC-665

ONE LAST RIDE

The clerk removed the eyeshade and hung it on a hook behind the postal cage, then adjusted his apron and sleeve garters as he once again became a storekeeper.

"Now, what is it that you will be needing today?"

Candler paused a moment to consider. "Do you have any of the paper cartridges for cap-and-ball revolvers?"

"I still carry some of those."

"Let me have a carton of the .36-calibers then, please. And a tin of percussion caps."

"Moving on, are you?" the clerk asked, his expression again saying louder than words that he disapproved of these itinerant cowhands who roamed here and there without any settled permanence.

"Something like that . . ."

Titles by Frank Roderus

THE WRANGLER
JUDGMENT DAY
SIEGE
DEAD MAN'S JOURNEY
WINTER KILL
LEFT TO DIE

MAN ON THE BORDER
OUTLAW WITH A STAR
(writing as Dave Austin)

THE
WRANGLER

FRANK RODERUS

BERKLEY BOOKS, NEW YORK

THE BERKLEY PUBLISHING GROUP
Published by the Penguin Group
Penguin Group (USA) Inc.
375 Hudson Street, New York, New York 10014, USA
Penguin Group (Canada), 10 Alcorn Avenue, Toronto, Ontario M4V 3B2, Canada
(a division of Pearson Penguin Canada Inc.)
Penguin Books Ltd., 80 Strand, London WC2R 0RL, England
Penguin Group Ireland, 25 St. Stephen's Green, Dublin 2, Ireland (a division of Penguin Books Ltd.)
Penguin Group (Australia), 250 Camberwell Road, Camberwell, Victoria 3124, Australia
(a division of Pearson Australia Group Pty. Ltd.)
Penguin Books India Pvt. Ltd., 11 Community Centre, Panchsheel Park, New Delhi—110 017, India
Penguin Group (NZ), Cnr. Airborne and Rosedale Roads, Albany, Auckland 1310, New Zealand
(a division of Pearson New Zealand Ltd.)
Penguin Books (South Africa) (Pty.) Ltd., 24 Sturdee Avenue, Rosebank, Johannesburg 2196,
South Africa

Penguin Books Ltd., Registered Offices: 80 Strand, London WC2R 0RL, England

This is a work of fiction. Names, characters, places, and incidents either are the product of the author's imagination or are used fictitiously, and any resemblance to actual persons, living or dead, business establishments, events, or locales is entirely coincidental.

THE WRANGLER

A Berkley Book / published by arrangement with the author

PRINTING HISTORY
Berkley edition / April 2005

Copyright © 2005 by Frank Roderus.

All rights reserved.
No part of this book may be reproduced, scanned, or distributed in any printed or electronic form without permission. Please do not participate in or encourage piracy of copyrighted materials in violation of the author's rights. Purchase only authorized editions.
For information, address: The Berkley Publishing Group,
a division of Penguin Group (USA) Inc.,
375 Hudson Street, New York, New York 10014.

ISBN: 0-425-20189-9

BERKLEY®
Berkley Books are published by The Berkley Publishing Group,
a division of Penguin Group (USA) Inc.,
375 Hudson Street, New York, New York 10014.
BERKLEY is a registered trademark of Penguin Group (USA) Inc.
The "B" design is a trademark belonging to Penguin Group (USA) Inc.

PRINTED IN THE UNITED STATES OF AMERICA

10 9 8 7 6 5 4 3 2 1

If you purchased this book without a cover, you should be aware that this book is stolen property. It was reported as "unsold and destroyed" to the publisher, and neither the author nor the publisher has received any payment for this "stripped book."

✦ 1 ✦

HIS BELLY RUMBLED and growled although he didn't know why. After all, he'd eaten just the day before.

The wagon climbed out of one rut and dropped into another with a bone-jarring thump. The impact dislodged a reel of bob wire from a stack of them and sent it rolling into the shins of one of the new hires. The man, the best dressed among the three of them, cussed and kicked the reel aside, sending it hard into the leg of the big fellow. The smaller man did not bother to apologize. The big fellow did not say anything either, although it must have hurt.

"Hey! You guys in the back. This up here is where you get out." They rolled on another seventy-five yards or so, then the driver pulled his team to a halt. "This is it. Follow those tracks there. They'll take you right to the Ladder."

The brand burned onto a board stuck upright beside the

turnoff read "III" and would naturally be known as the Ladder.

"Now, just a damn minute. You can't leave us out here in the middle of noplace." It was the smaller of Candler's two companions who spoke. The road disappeared behind a hogback. From here there was no sign of the ranch buildings.

"Mister, it's two miles over there and two miles back, and I got to put food on the table for seven hungry hands when I get back. I'm running late already."

"The hell you say. We can't carry our stuff all that far."

"Then set yourselves down and take root if you like, but I am not driving you over to the Ladder. Now, get the hell out of my wagon. You're trespassing."

By then Candler was already on the ground, along with his saddle and warbag. So was the big fellow and his gear. Finally, reluctantly, the third man got out of the wagon and lifted down a saddle, a bag and a small, hard-side trunk. With all that to tote, it was no wonder he wanted to ride, Candler thought.

"Thanks for your help," Candler told the driver. "Next time I see you in town, I'd like to buy you a beer."

"Aw, it wasn't nothing."

"Was to me. The offer stands." Candler picked up his kak and started walking. Normally with so far to go and a heavy saddle to carry, he would simply walk the two miles, get a horse at the ranch and come back for his things. But today he was curious about something.

He glanced behind, toward the main road where the

wagon belonging to a neighboring outfit was already in motion again.

The big man had shouldered his things and was trudging stolidly along, looking comfortable with his load. The other fellow was cussing and fuming, carrying his saddle and bag balanced awkwardly on one shoulder and dragging the trunk along the ground with his other hand. He was having a good deal of trouble trying to manage everything all at once.

Candler's expression did not betray any hint of the amusement he felt. Despite the smaller man's pushy manner, he hadn't thought for himself and left his gear, just followed Candler's example.

Candler turned his eyes toward the Ladder and briskly led the way.

"FELLA AT THE store in town sent us out here, ma'am. Said you're a widda lady and asked him to hire you some riders. I expect we're them. I'm Eddie Mannet, ma'am. I'm a top hand. I've worked cows from Texas all the way to Montana, and I'll see that the work gets done right. You can count on that."

Candler found it interesting that Mr. Mannet had virtually elected himself foreman. Interesting too that the lady did not challenge Mannet's assumption. Her business, of course. She was the boss; she was entitled.

"And who would you gentlemen be?" the lady in question asked. She was looking at the big man, who stood beside Mannet. Candler held back half a step.

The big man snatched his hat off. "M-ma'am?"

"What is your name please?"

"N-norman, ma'am. Shear. But I a-answer to most anything."

"Do you have experience working cattle, Mr. Shear?"

"Oh, yes, ma'am. I can work. I'm strong, ma'am. I can work good."

She smiled. "I am quite sure you can, Mr. Shear. I am very glad you will be working here."

Shear began to blush from that simple statement of confidence. Candler suspected that Shear was just a little soft in the head, the mind not a match for his muscles. Still, Candler knew of no reason why a simpleminded man couldn't be honest, and that was what counted more than anything else.

While the lady was going through all that, Candler was quietly studying her and the two buttons who stood close at her side.

The lady was likely somewhere in her thirties, a plain woman, thin, wearing what once had been a nice dress but now was stained and faded with age and long use. She was tall for a woman and had mouse brown hair peeping out around the edges of a gingham bonnet. She was not a woman men would turn to look at. But then someone had found her of interest, else she would not have had the two boys.

The older was probably ten, eleven years old. Thin like his mother, with fair hair and still with slightly girlish features. He would outgrow that eventually, but in the meanwhile Candler suspected this one was not popular with other boys his age. Likely they would tease and hound him. It was a subject John Candler knew something about.

The other boy was still in stockings and dresses. Three or maybe four. He held onto his mama's skirts with one hand and had the thumb of his other hand stuffed into his mouth. He too had fair hair and huge, very blue eyes.

"You, sir? Please introduce yourself."

"Yes, ma'am." Candler stepped out from behind Shear's shoulder and removed his hat so the lady could get herself a good look.

He gave her credit. She did not wince or turn away.

John Candler was not a handsome man. The right half of his face was marked with a dark, purple-black blotch that extended from his ear to the corner of his eye and down to the shelf of his jaw. His nose was thin and crooked, and the tip of it was missing. Apart from those disfigurements he was—or would have been—ordinary enough. Middle years. Middle height. Slight build. His hair was streaked with gray, as was the bushy mustache that hid his upper lip. His eyes were pale enough that had anyone ever cared to look closely they might have had difficulty deciding if they were blue or gray. Candler himself liked to think they were gray. But then he was a mite prejudiced in any choice between blues and grays.

He introduced himself and then stepped back into Norman Shear's shadow once again. The lady did not ask him about his experience or abilities. She directed her attention primarily to Mannet again.

"I am Catherine Wolbrough. These are my sons Donald," she indicated the older boy, "and James. My husband was caught in a blizzard on his way home one day last win-

ter. He froze to death." In town they said the husband had
been drunk at the time, but the lady did not mention anything about that.

She went on, "I am not of the West and I do not intend
to remain here. My task for you is to recover every cow or
calf or other animal that carries the Three I brand. I shall
sell them and take my sons back east where the three of us
belong. Until my cattle are found and sold, I will have little
to pay you. That is why you were hired at such a small
wage. Even at that, I will not be able to pay you all of it until a sale is made.

"Until then I shall pay each of you five dollars per
month in cash and give you a note for another ten. I will re-
deem the notes after the cattle are sold. I want that to be
clear to each of you. Do you understand that quite completely, Mr. . . . was it Manning?"

"Mannet, Miz Wolbrough. Eddie Mannet."

"Very well, Mr. Mannet. Do you understand what I have
told you?"

"Ma'am, Miz Wolbrough, I'm a top hand, like I told
you. I gener'ly get thirty a month an' keep."

"In that case, Mr. Mannet, I shall not be able to use your
services. I can pay only fifteen. I am sorry you went to all
the trouble of coming out here. Mr. Shear, do you understand that you will draw—"

"Ma'am, hold on now," Mannet interrupted. "I never
said I wouldn't want t' work for you. I'm a man as likes to
help a lady when I can. You know?"

She said nothing. Candler hid a thin smile. Perhaps

Mrs. Wolbrough knew and perhaps she did not, but there were no other jobs available anywhere in the basin. It was already too late in the season, and what jobs there were had already been filled.

"What are you telling me, Mr. Mannet?"

"I'm saying that I signed on t' ride for you, and that is what I expect I'll do. T' help you out, like."

"For fifteen dollars a month and part of that in the form of a note for collection later? Do you understand that, Mr. Mannet?"

"Yes'm."

"Mr. Shear?"

"Yes, ma'am." From his tone of voice Candler suspected Shear was merely answering to his name and not responding to the question that had been posed. Not that it probably mattered.

"Mr. Candler?"

"Yes, Mrs. Wolbrough, I understand the terms. I accept them."

"Thank you. There is a dugout over there beyond the corral. That will serve as a bunkhouse of sorts. I will do the cooking. You will take your meals in the house with me and my sons in the mornings and again at night. I intend to pack you bucket lunches to carry during the day. Please be so good as to return the buckets to me when you come in for supper each evening. I haven't buckets to spare."

She frowned. "I am sure there are a great many things I am neglecting to tell you, but I cannot think of what they might be. I shall tell them to you as they come to mind. All right? Please make yourselves at home in the bunkhouse. I will ring the steel when supper is ready. Oh, yes. There is a washbasin on the side of the house over there." She pointed. "Please use it before you come inside and wipe your feet on the rug on the stoop. Is there anything you want to ask?"

"No, ma'am, but I'll see to it that you get a good day's work outa us," Mannet assured her. "You can count on that."

"Thank you. Gentlemen." She bobbed her head and lifted her skirts and headed inside the house with the silent boys in tow—the little one literally so, the bigger one appearing a little reluctant to go.

"All right. You heard her," Mannet said in an authoritative tone. "Get your stuff an' follow me."

Meaning, Candler assumed, Mannet wanted to reserve first choice of bunk for himself.

Not that it mattered. He draped his saddle over a corral rail on his way past and carried his warbag into the dugout.

✦ 3 ✦

THE ACCOMMODATION WAS what one might call Spartan. Eddie Mannet's choice of wording was considerably more colorful than that. What either came down to was that there simply wasn't much to the living quarters provided on Mrs. Wolbrough's Ladder outfit. Or the Three I's as she seemed to prefer.

There was a dugout that very likely was the original homestead, a flat area carved out of a hillside and faced on the inside walls with flat stones laid up without benefit of mortar. The front wall consisted of a double layer of stone with dirt packed between the two. The roof was sapling-and-sod. Warm enough but prone to leak when the weather turned wet. The floor was packed earth. And there was a rusty steel camp stove at the back with a pipe leading up to a hole in the roof.

That was the extent of it. There were no bunks. No table or chairs. No stools. No lamps or lace curtains or doilies for the arms of the chairs that weren't there. No windows either, for that matter.

The entire affair ran ten feet deep into the hill by perhaps eighteen wide, ample floor room but a trifle on the bare side.

Whoever used to live there, the Wolbroughs or possibly someone before them, moved out completely when they left. Candler could see depressions on the floor that suggested there had been two beds, a table and some boxes or chests, but all that remained of any of them was some scrape marks where they were dragged away. Even the pegs in the wall, if there had been any, had been removed and taken elsewhere.

Not that any of that was important to him. Candler surveyed what little there was and carried his gear into a back corner. It would be warm there and dry and he had lived in worse conditions. Warm and dry could be considered quite good enough.

He dropped his warbag in the corner, untied and rolled out his blanket-lined patented canvas bed sack. And he was home.

While he was doing that, Norman Shear was doing much the same thing in the other rear corner. Eddie Mannet was still grumbling and cussing about comforts that did not exist. Eventually Mannet realized he'd squandered his opportunity to sleep close to the stove. He set up in one of the front corners, where the chill would seep through the stone if they were still living there come winter, and where the floor was apt to be the muddiest when the roof leaked. Mannet managed to give the impression that that was exactly where he'd wanted to be right along anyway.

There was no firewood and the nights were apt to be cold, so Candler went out to find the woodpile. There was little enough wood there and all of it needed splitting, so he poked through the lean-to built beside the corral to find a wedge and maul and busied himself splitting stove-lengths. He carried the first armload to the porch of Mrs. Wolbrough's cabin and left it there for the boy to find, then carried another back to the dugout and placed it beside the stove.

There was no kindling either so he went outside and used an ax to begin peeling splinters off a pine chunk, then worked some on reducing a tangle of slender logs into usable lengths with a bucksaw he found in the lean-to. The tools needed cleaning and the ax was in critical need of sharpening, but all in all the situation seemed tolerable enough.

Candler was still working on the woodpile when he heard the clang of the steel to call them to supper. By then his belly felt hollow and his head light, and he guessed he was ready enough for a meal.

✦ 4 ✦

THERE WAS A saying about hunger. Something about it lending flavor. Salt to the meat or . . . Candler could not recall the quotation, but he could certainly testify to its truthfulness. It was obvious at this meal that hunger could make the worst food palatable. That had to be so, because this was indeed the worst of foods.

Well, not so much that it was all that badly cooked. But it was so drab and starchy as to be as good as tasteless.

She fed them rice. And dandelion greens. And Salt. And . . . and that was that. There wasn't even vinegar to lend a little zing to the greens. Dandelion greens definitely need vinegar.

"Mighty good, ma'am, thank you," Candler said as he reached for a second helping of the rice and of the greens too and sprinkled salt liberally over all of it.

He understood well enough why she would feed this way. The woman was broke. Serious broke. It wasn't a case of her trying to feed on the cheap for her crew. She was feeding herself and her boys the same as the three hands.

"Thank you for having us in to your own table, ma'am. It's kind of you. Not necessary, of course, but mighty kind."

Shear mumbled something, grains of rice popping out of his mouth and decorating his shirt front when he spoke around a mouthful of grub. Candler assumed the big man was thanking Mrs. Wolbrough. Eddie Mannet picked at his food and ate only a little of the rice. He left the greens alone. That was fine, Candler thought. It left more for the rest of them. He reached for a third helping. The food lay warm and comfortable in his belly.

"I don't know which of you brought up the wood, but I do thank you," the lady said.

"We're glad to do what we can, missus," Mannet said, appropriating the credit for himself even though he hadn't lifted a finger to help with the woodpile.

"Tomorrow," she said, "I shall explain to you the extent of our range. I want all the cattle within those bounds gathered . . . rounded up, I should say . . . and brought in close to the ranch. We haven't any pasture under fence, so once we begin gathering the animals, one of you will have to watch them overnight lest they stray again. That will leave two to continue gathering."

"I will," Norman said quickly, surprising Candler. He hadn't seemed the sort to speak up much, and in fact he looked a little startled himself at his own audacity. He blushed slightly, his ears coloring and his already ruddy cheep taking on a warm red glow. "I, um, I like night. Riding alone. I can do that. Don't have to take turnabout."

"Excellent," Mannet declared. "Good man. Good of you to volunteer."

Mannet's enthusiasm suggested that he himself might not be so fond of riding all night long without relief on the herd and then trying to catch up on his sleep afterward as he could. That was the normal pattern if a nightherd was needed on a short crew. It made sense, though, to let Shear have it all, and then get his full measure of sleep during the days, if that was what the big man preferred. As far as Candler was concerned it was all work, no matter how you divvied it up.

"I shall have breakfast ready a half hour before dawn. In the meantime I would like you to pick out . . . what do you call them? Your string. I want you to choose your string this evening so you don't have to spend any time on it in the morning."

"We'll see to it right now," Mannet assured her.

"Very good then." She smiled. "I'm sorry that I haven't any dessert planned this evening. Are there any questions? No? Then I shall see all of you a little before daybreak. Good evening, gentlemen."

✣ 5 ✣

THE SADDLE STOCK were standing in a corral with their heads low and ribs showing. It was obvious that they hadn't been eating enough lately, not any more than the people around here did.

They seemed to have been living off the remnants of last year's piled hay, and the stack was down to the next thing to nothing. Candler guessed the woman was trying to stretch it out until the cattle were shipped, so she could sell the horses too and leave without having to waste time and money on cutting hay for a winter she did not intend to see.

There was nothing wrong with that as far as he was concerned. That was her privilege. But there was something seriously wrong with allowing good horses—or bad ones if these so proved to be—to go hungry when they were surrounded by a sea of good grass.

Candler began pitching a liberal helping of the old hay into the corral. The horses reacted like they hadn't eaten in quite a while. They fidgeted and snapped at one another but were too interested in the hay, or maybe too weak, to do any damage.

"If you throw all that hay, there won't be nothing left," Mannet warned, "and I dunno about you, but I'm not going out and mowing grass for anybody."

"Nobody will have to," Candler told him, "not any longer than she expects to need these horses. I saw a pile of old coal sacks in the shed over there and a spool of good twine. Figure we can twist up some of those sacks and make hobbles of them. Cut out the horses we want to use come morning and leave them in the corral with the hay and turn the rest out to graze. They won't go far. Not as hungry as they are and as tall as the grass is right close around the house."

Mannet grunted but did not argue. While he and Candler were talking, Shear was busy pumping water and carrying it to fill the trough inside the corral.

"Are you two ever going to quit fooling around with this other stuff and come pick your horses?" Mannet grumbled. "I want that tall bay over there."

The bay was the best-looking animal among the dozen or so—fourteen actually—in the bunch, but none of them seemed too bad. The dead husband must have known something about horseflesh when he got these together. Candler hoped they rode out as good as they looked.

The three men took turn and turnabout to pick out

horses that would be "theirs" for as long as they were on the Ladder, Shear choosing largely on the basis of size, obviously wanting horses big enough to carry him without breaking down, Mannet wanting the handsome looks and colorful markings, and Candler taking whatever he thought looked stout and serviceable. In the end all three seemed satisfied with the four horses they each chose.

"I think we should let those leftovers be," Candler suggested. "Mrs. Wolbrough or the oldest boy could be needing the use of a horse now and then. We'll leave those two in the corral for the family to get hold of easy."

"All right. All right, I suppose that sounds fair."

Candler went to fetch the empty jute sacks and twine so he could start making hobbles and turning horses loose. Shear hunkered down beside him and between the two of them they had the chore done and eleven horses out on the grass before the last lamp was extinguished inside the Wolbrough house.

"What about them fam'bly horses?" Shear asked as they headed back to the dugout, where Eddie Mannet's snores could already be heard.

"We'll bring them in come morning and leave them where she can get to them if she needs. In the meantime they can fill their bellies on fresh graze."

"We'll do that every right?"

"Yeah, I think it would be a good idea."

"I'll take care of it then. Bring those two in when I come in to sleep. You know?"

Candler nodded. He kind of liked Shear. The man was all right.

He felt his way to his bedroll in the dark and dropped gratefully onto it. Morning wasn't all that far away.

✢ 6 ✢

MORNING WAS FLAPJACKS, a dab of molasses and weak coffee. But it was food. It was hot. And Candler was pleased to have it.

"The Three I's controls the land for four miles in that direction," Mrs. Wolbrough said, pointing to the north "and about two miles or two and a half in the other three. Our cows should be there. There are some valleys and low hills, so the cattle can hide. Please be careful you don't miss any, won't you? I need every one you can find."

Candler lifted his coffee cup to his face to hide the smile that tried to betray his thoughts. Four miles in that direction, two in all the others, was it? That would be the day. The lady was nice, but she didn't know very much about cattle.

The Ladder range was not fenced. Not many outfits in

this part of the country were, although some were beginning to take it up nowadays.

During this past winter, especially with her dead husband not there to ride line and push them back, her beeves would've ranged to wherever they pleased.

And where they pleased would've been downwind. Once a cold wind got to blowing, they would have turned their tails into it, lowered their heads and drifted in front of the wind whichever way it carried them. Around here, he guessed, that would be south for the most part, east some of the time.

So where they needed to look for the Ladder bovines was south and southeast. There would be mighty few of them on the grass Mrs. Wolbrough thought she was using.

Likely they would be broken into pairs and small bunches and spread out for twenty or thirty miles downwind. And depending on the past winter, they could have drifted even farther, never mind what the lady expected.

"I have your lunches in these pails. Take one with you when you leave, please."

Candler wondered just where she'd thought her husband and any previous hands were off to in the years past when they rode out in the springtime to look for cattle. Just on that little patch of home range? Good grief, if they'd stayed within four miles or less the way she thought, they could've come to the house for their lunch every day.

The husband must have known what he was doing, for he had a nice place going here, but his wife sure hadn't paid any attention to her man's affairs.

Not that Candler figured it was any of his business. He was being fed here, and he would give the lady whatever work she required of him. That was the only thing he needed to think about. Just do an honest job of work. There was no need at all for him to worry about anything. Not anything at all.

At least that was what he thought at the time.

✢ 7 ✢

I T FELT GOOD to sit a horse again. Up high where a man could breathe and see the world around him, with all that power between his knees and secure in his hands. Candler sometimes felt like the thin ribbons of leather rein connected him straight to the horse's brain and made the two of them, horse and man, into something better than either one of them alone.

Of course there were times too when he was certain horses didn't *have* brains.

He laid the reins over to spin this one in a few circles, left and back right again, to sort of loosen him up and let them get to know each other, and the fool critter blew up complete.

Those ears went back. The head went down. The back curved up.

And Candler knew he was in for some morning exercise in the pale light of the dawning.

The tough little steeldust squealed and snorted, bucked and leaped, threw its head and reared up to paw the air and squeal some more. Candler wasn't sure, but he thought it was having itself some fun with all this.

That was all right. He never minded when a horse took a couple minutes to work out which was going to be the boss. And he was kinda enjoying it too. It had been weeks since he'd been on a horse. He'd missed it.

He took his hat off and let out a few yips like those exhibition riders did it, and after half a minute or so—it felt like an awful lot longer but he doubted that it was—the horse decided it was better to walk on all four legs and came back down to the ground again.

The horse blew once and shook itself like a dog coming out of water, and Candler figured the steeldust was ready for a day of work now. He leaned down and patted it alongside its neck and arranged the hair of the mane so it was all falling on the same side. The horse wasn't breathing particularly hard after shaking the kinks out, so he figured it had the staying power that he liked in a mount.

The others were sitting at the gate, Shear patient, Mannet seeming not to be.

"Are you done showing off?" Eddie Mannet snapped.

"If you boys aren't gonna buy tickets then I expect I'll have to be," Candler told him. He touched the steeldust with his heel, and the horse responded with its head up and ears forward as it stepped out all perky and eager.

They worked together comfortably enough to cut out the two horses they'd designated for family use and haze them back to the corral, leaving the remuda, what there was of it, out where the horses could continue to graze. Shear closed the gate, and Candler slipped down to the ground and flicked his reins over a fence rail so he could go inside the corral and take the hobbles off the pair of family horses. Then he swung onto the steeldust again and put it into a trot to join Mannet. The steeldust acted like it didn't even know what bucking was; it was that mannerly and gentle natured.

Not that Candler believed it, not for a minute. He smiled a little as he rode. He did like this horse. He surely did.

THEY RODE NORTH, just like Mrs. Wolbrough wanted, and they found cattle just where she said they would.

. They found XT cows and Fishhook cows and FR Connected Bar cows and 3J cows and . . . they found lots of cows. Not a single one of them was wearing the Ladder brand, of course, but they did find cows. Everything not wearing a Ladder burned onto its flank was turned back toward its home range—wherever that might be—which meant that they turned back every animal they encountered. Well, except for a few coyotes they spotted skulking in the brush. They didn't try to herd those anyplace, or rope them either, which could be fun to do but was hard on horseflesh.

"Tomorrow I'm gonna wear my pistols and collect me

some coyote pelts," Eddie Mannet declared when they stopped for their nooning. Neither Candler nor Norm Shear bothered to comment. Mannet was welcome to do whatever he pleased.

What Candler pleased was having lunch. Not that it was so much of a lunch, just cold biscuits with a smear of salted lard to take the place of butter, but it was better eating than he'd had in a while and he was glad to have it. He cleaned up every bit of what he'd been given. So did Shear. Mannet dumped part of his lunch out for the ants and birds to clean up and then bellyached that he was still hungry.

"I don't like the way that woman feeds us," Mannet complained. "A man deserves some decent food after a hard day's work."

Candler grinned. "Let me know when we get to the hard part, will you?"

"You know what I mean."

Candler nodded. "Sure I do, but for openers we haven't yet done a thing to earn our pay. Secondly, that lady doesn't have anything for her own self or her kids better than what she's giving us. And thirdly, by now she owes you a quarter of a dollar for your labor. Which I'm sure you can draw tonight if you think you can find something better."

"I was just talking, you know."

"Yes. I know."

Mannet kicked some dirt over the scraps of biscuit that he'd thrown away and said, "All right, pull your cinches tight and let's go. We need to find some of those Ladder beeves to take back with us tonight."

Not up in this direction, Candler thought as he stood and squatted down halfway a few times to loosen up his legs and get the blood to moving again. He said nothing, however. After all, Eddie was the foreman. Or so he seemed to think.

When they rode back to the house that afternoon, they had yet to see their first Ladder animal.

✛ 9 ✛

THE LADY WAS disappointed there were no cattle gathered in a full day of looking, but she tried to put the best face on things. She smiled and said something about tomorrow. Which was about all she could do under the circumstances, short of firing her three hands and trying to do the work herself.

Candler waited until Eddie Mannet and Norm Shear headed toward the bunkhouse, then took his hat off and approached the boss lady. "Ma'am, if it's all right with you, tomorrow we'll look where there's cattle."

She frowned. "I don't understand."

"You told us exactly where to look. We did. Now if you'd let us just go out and do what we think best, well, that might work a little better. If it's all right with you, that is. We'll all of us do exactly what you say."

"Oh. I . . . Yes, I'm sure that will be fine, Mr. Chandler."

"It's Candler, ma'am. Thank you." He bobbed his head and backed a step away before he put the hat back on and headed for the dugout.

Eddie Mannet was standing beside the corral with the two little Wolbrough boys. Mannet had a pair of six-guns strapped low on his waist and tied down on his legs with rawhide thongs. He was practicing fast draws, and the boys were wide-eyed and excited.

Candler drifted over that way and leaned against a fence rail to watch the show Eddie was putting on.

"Now this is the way you do it, see," he was telling the kids. "You stand with your feet just a little apart so you got a good base underneath you. See here what I'm doing? Shoulder width apart, that's the ticket. Then you get set. Hold your hands here. Like this. Elbow bent just a little and the wrist cocked. See? Then . . ."

Eddie's right hand flashed. His revolver practically leaped out of the holster. He was fast, all right. No question about that, Candler saw. The man could get a pistol out of the leather in a heartbeat.

And his pistols were pretty too. Nickel-plated and with ivory grips. Candler wasn't close enough to be sure, but he thought there was some engraving on the steel too. Handsome. Mannet must have paid an awful lot for those guns. Must value them awfully well too to still have them when he was out of work and out of food and close to out of hope, the way he'd been back there in town when the three of them agreed to sign on to work for the Ladder. Those guns meant a lot to him.

"You."

It took Candler a moment to realize Eddie was addressing him. He blinked. "Yes?"

"Ever see anybody faster than me?"

"No, I don't know that I have," Candler admitted.

That pleased Mannet. He smiled and grunted. "Damn right you haven't." He looked back at the boys. "Want to see that draw again? Lookee here now. Just like I showed you. Get your balance, see, and get set. Then," he went into a sort of crouch with his knees and elbows bent and curled his fingers like talons a few inches above the grips of the guns. The right-hand pistol flashed out of the leather and into his hand again. "Just like that. Just like that."

Mannet grinned, and the older Wolbrough boy—Donald, that was it, Donny—muttered something under his breath as he peered at this grown-up who was faster than lightning with a six-gun. The little one clung to his big brother's hand and looked around for something more interesting to catch his attention. A hawk or a kitten or something.

"I'm fast, aren't I?" Mannet asked Candler. "Well, aren't I?"

"Ayuh. You're fast, Eddie. Mighty fast."

Mannet drew his pistol again, more slowly this time, and spun it around on his index finger. Spun it several times and then dropped it back into his holster. Candler hoped the guns were not loaded. A dropped firearm was very apt to discharge if there was a cartridge under the hammer, and there was no telling which way an errant bullet might fly.

"You couldn't beat me, could you?" Mannet demanded. "Well, could you?"

"Me? Oh, I wouldn't know anything about that fast-draw stuff."

"Well, I do. Yessirree, I do." Mannet returned his attention to the boys and to his quick-draw practice.

Candler ducked his head to pass through the low doorway into the dugout. Shear was sprawled on top of his bedroll, snoring fit to bring the roof down.

Candler pulled his chaps and dropped them at the foot of his bedding. He thought there just might be time enough after supper this evening to build a bunk and peg it into the dugout wall. There were some scraps of discarded catch rope in the shed that he could use for springing. Sleeping in an actual bed might be kind of nice for a change.

✢ 10 ✢

THE MORNINGS WERE still chilly enough to make the water in the washbasin feel bracing. Invigorating. All right, colder than a witch's paps and fit to shiver a man right down to his socks. Candler splashed his face again and ran a hand over his chin, wondering if he should try to hack some of the stubble off or let it go awhile longer. He did not own a razor—had sold his to buy a sack of pinto beans and a palm of salt some weeks back—but his pocket-knife was pretty sharp.

Not that sharp, of course. No knife made will take the place of a good razor. But a man does with what he has.

What John Candler figured he had was a little more time. He would wait and maybe try to shave this weekend. He'd have more time to heal up then from the damage he expected to do to himself.

He washed his hands with a fingerful of the runny soap Mrs. Wolbrough had in a dish beside the washbasin, splashed his face one more time and then dabbed himself dry with the soft, many-times-washed flour sack that she'd put out for a towel.

"Are you done?"

"It's all yours," Candler told Norm Shear. The big man set in to wash himself. He seemed a pleasant fellow. Candler wondered if Shear had a razor he'd be willing to share.

"Mind if I ask you something?" Shear asked before Candler could inquire about the razor.

"Go ahead."

"How'd you make that bed of yours? I kinda like that. Like to make me one."

"I'll show you this evening after supper."

Shear grinned. "Thanks."

It was coming on toward daylight and Mannet hadn't yet shown himself outside the dugout.

Around at the front of the house Mrs. Wolbrough clanged the hanging iron, the clear, bell-like sound calling them to breakfast. Candler and Shear walked around to the front door. Eddie Mannet came bustling out of the dugout trying to finish pulling one boot on and tuck his shirttails in and smooth his hair back all at one time. He looked like he wasn't quite awake yet, and it was a wonder he didn't trip and fall and hurt himself.

Despite all that, he managed to be the first one inside,

and he had his bowl full of rolled oat porridge before either Shear or Candler got seated.

There was no sign of the little boys. Probably they were still in the loft sleeping.

"I do hope you find some of my cows today," the lady said as she poured some of the weak coffee that was heavily laced with chicory to make it go further.

"I think we will if we look down to the south and southeast," Candler said softly. "If you don't mind me sayin' so."

"That's what I was just about to say too," Mannet put in. "Yesterday we looked to the north. Today we will ride south."

"All right. I just hope you find something."

Candler grabbed for the pot of porridge. Shear had already taken most of it, and Mannet looked like he was about to go for seconds before Candler ever got the first glop of thick, gray stuff into his bowl. There was no sugar to sweeten it with but there was molasses and that was plenty good enough. The porridge lay warm and heavy in the stomach.

As before, Mrs. Wolbrough had three lunch pails set out. Each man took one on his way outside.

The three of them were saddled and on their way south before the bright disk of the morning sun got well up on the horizon.

✦ 11 ✦

THE COUNTRY WAS rougher than he'd thought. To the south it was choppy, all rocks and sharp angles, with pockets of brush and grass thrown in now and then. It was hard country to ride and harder to chase cows out of, but they found their first Ladder beeves, three barren cows, late in the forenoon, and after lunch managed to gather four more, two cows and a pair of half-grown calves that already carried Ladder brands. Wolbrough must have done some fall branding work before he came off that horse and froze to death.

"We'll start back now," Mannet announced once they had the cow and calf pairs out of the rocks.

It seemed a little early to Candler's way of thinking. But he wasn't going to stay out and work by himself.

Three men and seven beeves makes for kind of a small

herd. But it was a start. He hoped Mrs. Wolbrough would be encouraged to see some return on her investment of wages. Not that these animals were worth so terribly much, but they would more than pay for two days of work, and that was good. It was as it should be, for profitable beef was what made it possible for John Candler and men like him to earn a living as free men.

As they neared the Ladder headquarters, Candler bumped his horse into a trot and moved forward so he could announce to the others, "I'm gonna split off here and catch up with you at the house."

"Where the hell d'you think you're going?"

"I saw a blowdown over there. I want to drag some logs in for the woodpile. It's kind of low, and I used some of the poles last night when I was making my bed. We'll use some more this evening for Norm's."

"You're making him a bed?" Mannet snapped.

"No, he'll make his own bed. I just said I'd show him how. Do you want me to show you too?"

"I know how to build a damn bed."

"Yeah, I'm sure you do," Candler mumbled under his breath as he reined away and headed toward the gully where he'd spotted that blowdown earlier. He intended to drag a little of the wood in now, and if there was time later on, he could bring the wagon out and get a proper load. The lady could not afford coal to fire her stove so she would be needing wood to burn instead, and the only cost for the wood would be a little sweat.

Candler figured he had plenty of that to offer.

He lifted his horse into a lope and left Mannet and Shear to finish pushing the cattle back onto the Ladder's home grass.

✛ 12 ✛

"WHAT'CHA DOIN', MISTER?"

Candler looked up from the stub of wood he was chopping with a hatchet, shaping it to make an end post for Norm Shear's bed. A long side rail and shorter end rail would be fitted into the walls on one end of each and into this corner post at the outside foot of the bed. A network of rope latticed between the rails and the walls would serve in place of springs. Candler smiled at the two boys and explained.

Donald made a face. "That isn't very interesting."

"No, I suppose not. Unless you happen to need a place to sleep. Then it becomes interesting."

"My bed," Shear told the boys proudly. He was using an ax to smooth what would become the foot rail. The big man seemed pleased with himself.

The boy gave both of them a rather haughty sniff and went off to look for Eddie Mannet, who was once again out behind the shed practicing his quick draw with the six-guns.

Mannet carried two guns, Candler noticed, but he only ever took the right one out. The left, he supposed, was there as a backup. Like if he emptied the cylinder in the first gun and still hadn't managed to hit what he was shooting at.

Candler smiled a little and chided himself for being catty. He'd never seen Mannet actually shoot, and for all he knew the man might be aces.

Or not.

Not that it mattered.

"Don't trim that point down too fine," he advised Norm. "Don't forget that it is the part that will have to carry your weight."

"Is this good?" Shear held the length of pine up for Candler to see.

"Real good on that end. Now a little more on the end that fits into this notch, and we'll go put it all together."

Shear grinned and resumed very delicately removing slivers of wood from the end of the short rail.

✦ 13 ✦

"THANK YOU FOR the wood, whichever of you split it," Mrs. Wolbrough said at breakfast the next morning. All three of them muttered the obligatory "you're welcome" comments even though Eddie Mannet had not yet acquainted himself with the woodpile.

"Donald, you can stand watch over the cows today while Mr. Shear gets some sleep. He rode around them all last night after working all day too, so he must be tired." She put her spoon down and looked at Norm. "Mr. Shear, would you please take a few minutes before you sleep to show Donald what must be done to hold those cows together?"

"Yes'm." Norm looked proud to have been told to teach something to someone else. Not particularly bright himself, it was quite possibly the first time in his life he had been asked to do something like that, and he carried the instruction like a badge of honor.

"Mr. Mannet, I should like for you to stay here for a moment when the others leave to begin working this morning. There are some things we need to discuss, you and I."

"Yes, ma'am. Whatever it is, I'll take care of it," Mannet assured her.

Candler finished his meal in silence, excused himself and went outside into the cool of the dawning. The sky to the east was streaked with violet and gold so that it looked like the heavens were on fire. This was perhaps his favorite time of day, and he stood in the yard for a minute enjoying it while he waited for Norm and the boy to catch up. Then the three of them tramped off to the corral without waiting on Mannet.

Twenty minutes later Candler watched as the horse Eddie Mannet chose for the day got its morning exercise, warming its muscles at Eddie's expense with a little bucking and snorting.

"Playful," Candler observed once Eddie had the animal standing with all four feet on the ground.

"I'll give the son of a bitch 'playful.' If it keeps that up, I'll beat it down to its damn knees. Then it won't be feeling s'damn playful." Mannet's tone of voice made it clear he was not joking.

"It was only getting the kinks out," Candler said softly. "Most any horse will do that."

"This one better not," Mannet said. He jabbed the horse

with his spurs, then pulled hard against the bit when it jumped forward. "Walk, damn you, walk."

The horse came back down to a walk, and Candler squeezed his own mount forward to go along with the self-appointed foreman. Or it could be that Eddie was now officially the foreman. Candler suspected that was what Mrs. Wolbrough wanted to tell him back there.

Now that he'd had the thought, his curiosity built. Fully expecting to hear that Eddie Mannet was now the boss of the hands—such as they were—he asked, "What did the boss lady want of you?"

"The bitch wanted to mess in my personal business, that's what she wanted," Mannet snarled.

"Geez, I'm sorry. I didn't mean to bring up anything personal. I kinda assumed it was ranch business she was telling you."

Mannet acted like he hadn't heard the apology. "Know what she told me? She doesn't approve of guns. Can you believe that? Rough as this country is? And she don't approve of guns?

"Said the boy is all gaga over me bein' so fast with my irons. Well hell, of course he is. You ever see a kid that wasn't interested in such stuff? Of course you haven't. Won't neither. But that bitch back there, she says she don't approve of guns and don't want any on her damn property. Well, you can believe that I told her better'n that. Told her if she wants my guns off her place then she's telling me to get off too. She could pay me off then and there or she could shut her damn mouth about me and my guns. I'll do whatever I please, and that's that."

Candler suspected Mannet was giving him a carefully colored account of the conversation. But he could believe that the lady did not know or understand firearms and therefore feared them. He could also believe that she did not want to lose any of the few hands she'd been able to find who were desperate enough for work that they would accept her terms of employment. Likely she settled for a promise that Mannet would keep his revolvers locked away while he was on the Ladder.

Heck, a good many outfits kept a sturdy locker for exactly that purpose. New hires were required to deposit their weapons in a trunk or cabinet where they would be held under lock and key until the hand drew his time and left the spread. Some did not even allow their people to carry firearms to town when they had days off, although hunting excursions were generally allowed. Ranch owners, though, found there was much less violence, or at least less serious injury, when gunpowder was kept out of the picture.

"She ain't gonna tell me what to do," Mannet declared after a minute or two of silence. "I can tell you that much. She might be my boss but she ain't my keeper."

Candler said nothing.

They rode south again to hunt for more of the Ladder beeves. The ranch books said there should be several hundred of them somewhere out there. For the lady's sake and that of those kids, Candler hoped they would be able to find and ship the entire bunch of them.

✢ 14 ✢

Six DAYS AND seventeen beeves later Mannet surprised Candler when after breakfast he declared, "We aren't hunting cows this morning."

"I thought that's what we were here for."

"We are, but not this morning. That woodpile is getting too low. Today we're gonna take the wagon and go cut some wood. You know where the harness is. Hitch them two into it. I'll put hobbles on these others. We won't be using them."

"All right." Candler suspected there was more than one reason why Eddie Mannet wanted to replenish the woodpile. All the long, slender poles had long since either been sawed into short lengths or used to make beds for Candler and for Norm Shear. Mannet was still sleeping on the floor, and if he wanted to make a bed for himself he needed to find poles to build it.

The man hobbled the pair of saddle horses Norm had hazed into the corral when he came in from riding night herd on the cattle, the two intended for use by Mannet and Candler. When he was done with that chore, Mannet disappeared into the dugout and came out seconds later carrying his gunbelt. He stowed it beneath the wagon seat, then grabbed an ax and the big bucksaw out of the shed.

By that time Candler had a team in harness. He backed the horses onto the wagon tongue and hooked the traces on. He sorted out the driving lines and wrapped them around the empty whip socket.

Mannet was over by the corral having a word with the boy. After a moment the Wolbrough boy grinned and waved and cantered off toward the bed ground where Norm had left the cattle earlier.

"Ready?" Mannet asked when he reached the wagon.

"I am." Candler placed his lunch bucket under the wagon seat beside Mannet's guns.

Eddie climbed into the driver's seat and took up the lines. "Get up here then."

"Are you sure you wanta go now?"

"Hell yes. Now, quit dawdling."

"Fine." Candler stepped onto the axle and then into the driving box. He settled onto the seat beside Mannet. "But if I was you, I think I'd take my lunch along."

Mannet looked startled. Then angry. "You could've got it for me."

"Could've," Candler agreed. "Didn't."

"Damn you," Mannet sputtered. "Damn you, I . . ."

Candler looked at him. "You what?"

Mannet looked away. "I don't much like you, Candler."

Candler did not bother to answer. After a moment Eddie Mannet climbed back down off the wagon and went to fetch the lunch pail he'd left sitting beside the corral gate.

✦ 15 ✦

THE RANCH HORSES were skittish in harness; they were accustomed to being under saddle instead. If the Ladder had any heavy horses when the mister was alive, they were gone now. Sold off perhaps to provide a few dollars of operating capital. Or perhaps some of the lighter horses were trained to pull and Mrs. Wolbrough just didn't know to tell them.

Still, the animals settled down after a couple miles and pulled more or less together after that.

It was funny perhaps, but Candler felt a mite skittish himself when he was riding behind pulling horses. He was much happier on top of one animal where he could take charge if need be with hands, feet, shift of weight, whatever it took.

Horses in harness were under the flimsy control of just

the driving lines, and if they spooked, they could take a notion to run out of control. A wagon wreck was a terrible thing to see and could cause serious hurt. Candler had had about as much hurt as he wanted.

He found his hand rising to lightly touch the side of his face when he got to thinking about that. Then, catching himself at it, he glanced to the side to see if Eddie Mannet noticed. He didn't think so.

They passed the open end of a shallow swale where Candler remembered seeing a tangle of a long-ago blow-down, and he asked, "Where're we going?"

"What's it matter to you?" Mannet snapped, apparently still peeved because Candler hadn't been willing to play fetch for him back at the house.

"Nothing. Just curious." Candler hushed up and sat back to enjoy the ride. Which was not exactly an easy thing, as they were traveling cross-country, not on a road, and the wagon was bumping and bouncing worse than a bad horse on a cold morning. At least on horseback a man could cling with his legs too. Riding on a wagon seat, he found himself being thrown off the bench about as much as he was sitting down on it.

Mannet took them into the string of low hills lying west of the Ladder and climbed toward a stand of aspen that lay spilling down off the crest of one of the taller hills.

The grade wasn't too awfully steep, but had Candler been driving, he would have snake-tracked back and forth a little to make the climb easier on the horses. Mannet just pointed them up and made them pull. Not that it was too terribly difficult for them. The wagon was empty save for the men and the tools. It was enough of a climb, though, to get their nostrils flared and chests heaving by the time they reached the aspen.

Mannet swung the rig in a wide half circle and stopped when it was pointed downhill. Candler jumped down without waiting to be told and found some rocks that he could use to brace the wheels against rolling. A hand brake is a dandy thing, but only a fool would trust one.

He gathered up the lines and secured them into a tight skein of leather ribbons so they would not get underfoot, then unhitched the team and led them away from the wagon before he slipped hobbles on and stepped very gingerly away.

He wasn't sure how the horses would act, being hobbled while still in harness, but all they did was drop their heads and begin cropping the pale, wiry grass.

Eddie Mannet, he saw, had buckled his gunbelt on and was practicing his fast draw again.

"There's only one ax," Mannet said. "You go ahead and drop some likely looking trees. Once you get them limbed, I'll bring the horses and drag them down to where we can load 'em."

Candler was careful to keep his annoyance from showing. Even if Mannet had been properly named the boss—which he hadn't—it was one thing to be boss and another thing completely to be bossy.

Still, it wasn't worth fighting about.

But then not many things were, Candler believed.

He let the tailgate down, got the ax from the back of the wagon and walked uphill to the aspen grove to begin cutting.

✢ 16 ✢

"Somebody's coming," Candler announced. He straightened up and leaned backward, then from side to side, and finally twisted at the waist, left and right and left again, trying to work some of the kinks out of his back. It was hard work chopping the limbs off the felled tree trunks, and sweat was running into his eyes. He'd long since taken his hat off and laid it on the wagon seat. The heavy felt hat only made him feel hotter. Not that the sun on his bare head was cool. It was one of those deals where there weren't any good choices so about all a man could do was to make the one that was less bad than the other and go on about his business.

In this case his business was sweating and aching. Or so it seemed at the moment.

"Huh?"

"I said somebody's coming," Candler repeated. He pointed.

Down on the flat below he could see a dark figure moving through the grass. From this distance the horse and rider looked no bigger than an ant.

"That's the kid," Mannet said. "I told him to ride up here at lunchtime."

"What for?"

"Is that any of your business?" Mannet said.

"Maybe not, but those cows we've been gathering sure are. If he isn't watching them, who is? I don't want to have to go find them a second time."

"The cows will stay put."

"Sure. If you say so."

"What do you mean by that?" Mannet demanded.

Candler ran the back of his wrist over his forehead to drag some of the sweat away and keep it from getting down into his eyes. He said nothing. The reason Eddie Mannet was so waspish about it, Candler figured, was that Mannet knew he was in the wrong to be taking the boy away from his job.

At least the visit was prearranged, and so the boy was not riding out to tell them about some emergency back at the ranch. That was something.

"We'll knock off now," Mannet said. Donny was a good half hour away and they could have gotten some more work done until he arrived.

"You go ahead. I'm gonna finish this one that I've got started."

Mannet gave him a sharp look but said nothing. He walked over to the wagon and retrieved the gunbelt he'd taken off earlier when he finally got around to doing some work, using the Swedish saw to cut up the logs that Candler dropped and limbed. Now he buckled the belt around his waist again and made a few more practice draws. For a change he even tried drawing with his left hand too. He was much slower with that hand and handled the heavy revolver awkwardly when he did get it out.

Candler picked up the ax—the edge could use some work with the Arkansas stone; he could do that during the lunch break, he figured—and went back to slicing the thin, whippy limbs off the aspen trunk.

✢ 17 ✢

THE KID MADE the long jump down off his horse—in order to get on, he had to use an extra stirrup hanging down low and climb it like a ladder up the side of the horse—and tied his animal to a wagon wheel.

"Am I too late?" He sounded eager.

"No, I been waiting on you."

"Really? Gee, thanks, Mr. Mannet. Thanks a lot."

Candler took the ax with him. He collected his lunch pail out of the driving box, then carried it and the ax around to the back, deposited them there and went back to the front to get the rag-wrapped package that held a small screw-top tin of whale oil and the flat Arkansas stone.

He also got his hat and put it on. It was still hot even when he wasn't swinging the ax, but he just wasn't comfortable without a hat on his head. Pure habit, that was all.

He hopped up onto the tailgate and opened the lunch pail. Corn cakes and salted lard. No surprise there. But it was food, honestly earned, and he was grateful to have it.

Eddie Mannet and Donny ignored him. No surprise there either.

Mrs. Wolbrough had packed a half dozen of her light and crumbly corn cakes. They would have been better if they'd been a little moist, but she always cooked them dry. And without the touch of sweetener that separates an ordinary corn cake from an excellent one. Candler was tempted sometimes to show her how to make them, but he never did.

He ate the first one, then pulled the ax into his lap and ran a thumb over the edge. He began the slow, patient task of putting a proper edge on the blade, finding his angle and then scrubbing the steel with the grit of the Arkansas stone.

He would stroke for a while, then chew a little, then go back to the ax again. His sweat began to dry and the sun felt good on his back. High overhead a pair of eagles danced in the sky.

Mannet and the boy walked a little way off from the wagon. Candler saw Mannet take his left-hand pistol out and hand it to the boy.

They were too far away for Candler to hear what they were saying. But he didn't need to. He could pretty much tell just from watching. Mannet was showing the gun to the boy, pointing out the different parts and what it was that they did.

He thumbed the hammer halfway back and flicked the

loading gate open and spun the cylinder around, holding it so the boy could see into the empty chambers.

Then Eddie slid half a dozen fat, brass cartridges out of the loops on his gunbelt and fed four of them into the chambers, rotating the cylinder to admit each one in turn. He said something and Donny held his hand out so Mannet could put the last two cartridges into his palm.

Eddie handed the gun to him and the boy rather awkwardly loaded the last two chambers, his face a study in intense concentration.

Mannet nodded and said something and the boy grinned. Eddie took the revolver back and dropped into what Candler had come to think of as Eddie's gunfighter stance. He cocked the pistol and raised it, aiming into the sky. He must have been aiming at one of the eagles, but knew good and well he couldn't hit it. After a second or so he said something to the boy and brought his attention back down to earth, this time aiming the gun at something, a rock or a chunk of wood or some such, on the ground.

The fancy Colt barked, the sound of it dull and hollow, and Donny squealed and covered his ears. But the boy was grinning.

Eddie fired three times more, then said something and handed the gun to Donny.

The kid needed both hands to hold the revolver more or less steady. Except for that his posture was a smaller copy of Eddie's.

The gun boomed again and the boy like to dropped it. He didn't, though, and was steadier with the sixth and final shot. Candler couldn't see if either one of them hit anything.

But then that wasn't the point. Candler figured it was damned decent of Eddie to be teaching the boy like that, even if it had taken Donny away from the cows for way too long.

The two of them, man and boy, talked a little longer, then came over to the wagon where Eddie got his lunch pail. Donny wandered around to the back of the wagon and stood watching Candler work on the ax, taking in the way it was done but not asking questions or saying anything.

"Hey, kid. Come up here." Mannet pointed to the seat of the wagon, and Donny trotted away and climbed up there beside his idol. Candler continued sharpening the ax blade while he munched on the last of his corn cakes.

✠ 18 ✠

"STAY A MOMENT, please," Mrs. Wolbrough said as her hired hands were finishing supper.

Candler nodded and laid his spoon down. Supper had been pinto beans cooked like a thick soup with some flakes of salt pork thrown in for extra flavor. Some peppers and maybe a little onion would have been nice, but he'd enjoyed it the way it was and had no complaints.

Mannet finished directly and then they all sat and waited for Norm to be done. Shear had an appetite that was at least as big as he was. There were never leftovers when he walked away from the table. If Mrs. Wolbrough wanted to cook anything ahead of time, she had to leave it off the table or Norm would clean it right up. Candler sometimes wondered just how much grub Norm could put away if he were ever given free rein to eat all he could handle.

Once the bowl of bean soup was empty, Norm quit eating, wiped his face and hands with the flour sacking Mrs. Wolbrough always gave each of them for napkins, and sat patiently with his hands folded waiting for the boss lady to speak her piece.

"You said you wanted us to stay?" Mannet asked.

"Yes, thank you. Boys, you are excused. Donald, please take your brother outside. Wash his face and hands for me, please. Then take him up to the loft and get him into his nightshirt if you would."

"Yes, Mama." Donny looked disappointed that he would not be able to hear everything that was being said. He took his little brother by the hand, though, and led James out to the washstand.

"You three have been working very hard for the past two weeks. I know that and I appreciate it. Tomorrow you may take the day off. If any of you wishes, you may each have an advance against your pay of two dollars. Naturally if you do not want your pay yet, you will receive it at the end of the month. Just let me know."

"I'd like mine now," Mannet said quickly.

"Mr. Shear?"

"Yes'm."

"Mr. Chandler?"

"It's Can . . . uh, never mind. I expect I'll take mine now too."

"Very well then." She stepped behind the blanket which, suspended from a rope like an indoor clothesline, served to partition off a part of the cabin. She emerged a moment later and starting with Eddie Mannet counted four silver half dollars into each man's hand.

She also produced a paper, already made out, stating that each of the undersigned had received two dollars cash in hand.

"Please sign this, each of you."

She found a bottle of ink and a pen with a patented steel nib, and each of them signed. Candler was a little surprised that big Norm could write his name. He did it slowly and with great concentration, but his letters were carefully formed and perfectly rounded. Someone had gone to great lengths to teach Shear that penmanship, Candler guessed. Someone who must have cared about the big man very much in order to be as patient as the task must have required.

Donny and James returned while the pen and ink were passing around the table. Donny took his little brother up the ladder into the loft where the boys slept.

"Very well, then," Mrs. Wolbrough said when Candler had signed too. "I will expect you back here for breakfast the day after tomorrow. Please be so good as to return in a fit condition for working."

"Yes'm."

"Yes, ma'am."

There was a scraping of chair legs as the men got up from the table. Candler could see Donny at the top of the ladder peering down through the opening into the loft. He looked like he was hoping to be invited to spend the free time with Mannet, but Eddie did not look in his direction.

Candler could see the disappointment keen in the boy's face when Mannet walked away. Shear and Candler followed him out.

"I'm goin' to town tonight," Mannet declared. "Norm, loan me one of them dollars."

The big man shook his head and gave Eddie a hard look.

"What about you, Candler?"

"No, I don't expect so."

Mannet cussed the both of them and went to the dugout to get his guns. Shear ambled toward the corral.

"Are you going in tonight too, Norm?"

"Got to work. The lady said we're off tomorra. She didn't say nothing 'bout me taking tonight off. I got cows to tend."

Candler nodded. He himself went over to the woodpile. He intended making a good fire tonight and thought it only fair to replenish what he burned up.

Eddie Mannet had dressed and gone by the time Candler cut and split two armloads of stove-lengths, one for the house and the other for his own fire. Norm had saddled and gone out to keep watch over the small herd they'd managed to assemble thus far, leaving Candler with the dugout all to himself.

✢ 19 ✢

PEACE, QUIET AND having only his own odors to contend with were mighty pleasant for a change. Candler built a door-busting fire in the little stove and set a pot of water on to heat.

He stripped down to the skin and felt of his face. He was halfway toward growing a beard, and he did not like beards. He'd tried years ago to wear one, thinking it would cover the scars on his face. Unfortunately a beard only seemed to emphasize them. And make it look like he was trying to cover them over. Besides, a beard just did not feel good to him, never mind what he looked like when he wore one.

He did not own a razor of his own, and the Ladder should have supplied a razor and strop for the hands. Mrs.

Wolbrough wouldn't know that. It was annoying though. A little. The shave would just have to wait.

Candler found a piece of rag that he could use for a washcloth and rubbed some of Mrs. Wolbrough's runny soap onto it. Soap and warm water felt marvelous. As invigorating as a spring rain. He washed himself all over, rinsed out the rag and wiped himself down with the wet cloth, then rinsed several times more until he felt thoroughly clean. By then the water was almost too hot to touch. Normally he would have set the pan off the stove and let it cool, then stepped outside to pour it over himself. He wasn't sure Mrs. Wolbrough would understand that likelihood though. There was quite a bit she didn't know about having hands on a place. Her husband could have told her except for the inconvenience of him having died in that snowstorm.

He used his clean shirt to dry off with, then with a shrug stuffed his dirty shirt and socks and underdrawers into the pot and drizzled a little soap into it too. He used a stick of starter wood to slosh things around in there, then moved the pot to the back of the stove. By morning the stove would have burned itself out and the water would have cooled. He could wring his clothes out and hang them over a fence rail, and that would take care of his laundry requirements for a spell.

He pulled his one pair of clean underdrawers on and stretched out on the bunk he'd built for himself, luxuriating in the comfort of being alone. It was too warm inside the dugout, but that was a small price to pay for the other comforts he was finding here.

Candler closed his eyes and made the most of his time off in that most time honored of methods. He slept.

✣ 20 ✣

"**M**ORNIN', NORM."

"Mornin', John." Shear dismounted, pulled his saddle and hung it on the corral rail, then hobbled the horse he'd been using for nightherd and turned the animal loose. He slipped inside the corral, where Candler was saddling a horse and shook out a loop in his catch rope.

"You aren't going to get some sleep before you head for town?" Candler asked.

Shear grinned and shook his head. He made a clumsy throw that fell over the head and neck of another of Norm's string. That was something Candler had noticed about Norm. He did things awkwardly, but he got them done. That was what counted.

Candler drew his cinches just tight enough to keep the saddle from slipping under the horse's belly, then waited for Norm to finish putting a saddle on his day mount. The two of them walked together to the house, washed and then went inside.

"Ma'am." Candler bobbed his head and hung his hat on a peg beside the door. He nudged Norm in the side and pointed with his chin to remind the big man to remove his hat too.

"Will Mr. Mannet be joining us for breakfast?"

"No, ma'am. He went on in to town already."

"And will any of you be here for lunch today or dinner this evening?"

"No, ma'am, I wouldn't expect so."

"Very well, but if you do come back, please let me know so I can cook enough for all of us."

"Yes, ma'am. Is there anything you need for us to bring from town for you?"

She looked for a moment as if she would speak, her plain features brightening almost into a smile. Then the brief change of expression subsided and she shook her head. "No. Thank you for offering. I wouldn't want to bother you on your day off."

"No bother, ma'am. If there's anything you need, I'd be glad to do it."

"Quite certain about that, are you?"

"Yes, ma'am, I am."

"Very well then. I could use a spool of cotton thread. Black. No, make that two spools. Get white as well, if you would. And a paper of needles. I need to begin thinking about what my boys will wear when we travel back east. I can make over some of my . . . some of my husband's shirts and things for them. Would you mind doing that for me?"

"Wouldn't mind at all."

Norm was already seated at the table waiting for Mrs. Wolbrough to set the porridge down. Overhead in the loft there was a stirring of thumps and half-heard voices as the boys began to get awake. Generally Mrs. Wolbrough served the men their morning meal before the boys came downstairs. She filled each man's bowl then put more into a serving dish, holding back some in the cooking pot. Candler assumed that would be her breakfast and that of her sons.

She had cooked enough for three hungry men, which suited Norm Shear just fine. He ate Eddie Mannet's share in addition to his own. A man had to step lively to see to his own interests when Norm was around, at least as far as food was concerned.

"We might be late getting back," Candler told her when he and Shear rose to leave. "I'll bring your thread by in the morning. Unless you need it tonight. I can come back early if you like."

"That will not be necessary, Mr. Chandler, but I thank you."

"Yes, ma'am." There seemed no point at all in trying to convince her that his name was Candler. Not at this late date. "Tomorrow morning then."

Donny was coming down the ladder as the men left. He was dressed and presumably would be riding day herd as usual today. The little guy, James, was still in his nightshirt.

Big brother came down ahead of him, poised to catch
James if he should take a tumble. Donny wasn't a bad kid,
Candler thought.

He put his hat on and touched the brim to Mrs. Wolbrough, then followed Norm out to the corral to pull the
cinches snug and head to town with two dollars cash
money in their pockets.

✦ 21 ✦

I T WASN'T EXACTLY a blowout, but it was a nice change
from working anyway. Candler lifted the tin mug, heavy
with liquid, and took a deep, welcome, throat-cleansing
swallow of the beer. He reached for a chunk of rat cheese
and another of the hard, dried-out ham from the free lunch
counter. After a steady diet of porridge, hotcakes and corn
dodgers, the cheese and the meat were mighty welcome.

He understood that the dry, crumbly cheese and heavily
salted ham were intended to increase a man's thirst so he
would want to drink more of the highly profitable beer.
That was all right by him. And in fact he probably would
have another beer later on. In the meantime it was nice to
put an elbow on the bar and a boot on the foot rail and just
relax for a bit.

Norm was already nose down in his second beer and

looked like he would be content to stay here for the rest of the day.

Eddie Mannet was over in the corner at a card table with four other fellows. He must have been doing pretty well with the pasteboards because he had a bottle of whiskey at one elbow and a fat girl with henna red hair at the other. Mannet hadn't bothered to acknowledge either Shear or Candler when they arrived.

Candler smiled a little. Probably Eddie was afraid if he said anything to them it could be taken as an invitation or, worse, a friendly overture, in which case they might want to borrow some of his winnings. Candler took another swallow of the beer.

He kept looking to see if he could spot the cook from the next outfit south, the J3Y. He'd promised to buy the man a beer for that ride he'd given all of them. Candler had not forgotten that obligation.

He had more of the cheese and a pickled egg and drank off the rest of his beer.

"Another?" the barman asked.

Candler shook his head. "Not yet. But I'll be back directly."

"We'll still be here," the bartender assured him.

"Are you gonna go see the sights, Norm, or will you be staying here?"

"Sights? What for sights is there?"

"It's just an expression, Norm. A . . . Never mind. I'll see you later."

Norm nodded and signaled to the barman to bring his

third beer. Let's see, Candler thought. Norm had two dollars. Twenty beers to the dollar. Yeah, he expected that Norm had enough in his pocket to get himself right thoroughly drunk even if he could hold the stuff well. Liquid happiness. And maybe drag back fifty cents for that other kind of a cowhand's recreation. But then why not. Every now and then a man wanted to feel something other than tired.

Candler nodded a thank-you to the bartender and went outside, force of habit prompting him to tilt his hat over at a jaunty angle that just happened to also drop the brim so that it put the dark scars on his face into shadow.

For a while there, out at the Ladder where there were just the few of them and the others all accustomed to looking in his direction without really seeing him, he had forgotten the reactions he caused in strangers. Here in town he was sometimes reminded of it.

✛ 22 ✛

"**M**R. EBBERSLEY." CANDLER nodded. "How are you today?"

"Fine, thank you. Let me see now. You're one of the fellows I sent out to the Ladder a few weeks ago, is that right?"

"You have a good memory," he told the shopkeeper.

"Do any good out there?"

"Yes, sir. I have a job. Food. Bed. That's more'n I had when I got here."

Clinton Ebbersley nodded. "That's good. She needed the help." He smiled and wiped his hands on his apron. "In that case I know you aren't here looking for work. What can I do for you today, friend?"

"I need a paper of sewing needles. Steel ones, please." Candler paused to consider. He had needles in his warbag, big ones sturdy enough that he could sew a calf's ear or a pair of torn britches, either one. The needles came four to the paper, and if he remembered correctly he still had two left so didn't need any more for himself. And he still had some thread too. Mrs. Wolbrough, though, would want the smaller needles. She would be sewing light cloth and not some animal's hide. And she would want regular thread, not the heavier stuff Candler and most cowhands of his acquaintance favored.

"What gauge needle?" Ebbersley asked.

"Gauge?" Candler had no idea what the man meant.

"What size?"

"Oh, uh . . . 'bout this long." He showed Ebbersley what he meant with his thumb and forefinger. "It's for making shirts and like that."

"Of course. Anything else?"

"Yes, sir. I need two spools of cotton thread. One white, one black."

"What weight?"

Candler looked blank.

"Big spool or little one? Thread for those shirts or thread for repairing a torn boot?"

"Big spools, I think. Little thread. For shirts and stuff."

"I'll be right back." Ebbersley left the counter and rummaged on a shelf over at one side of the store. He was back a moment later with a black paper folder that would hold the needles and the two big spools of 'little' thread. "What else?"

"I think that's everything, Mr. Ebbersley."

"All right. That will be twenty-eight cents."

"You can put it on Mrs. Wolbrough's bill. Catherine Wolbrough. You know. At the Ladder where I'm working."

Ebbersley's expression changed. Hardened. At first Candler did not understand why.

The shopkeeper laid his hand over the thread and needles on the counter and pulled them back away from Candler.

"Is something wrong?"

"No more credit. I'm sorry. I already told her that. I can't extend her any further credit until she pays me what she already owes."

"We're getting the cows gathered. End of summer, sir, we'll take them down to the railroad for her. There will be buyers there. You know there will. The lady will have cash money then. In the meantime she's pretty well strapped."

"I am truly sorry, mister, but this is a discussion I've already had with her several times over. I relented the last two times. I can't do that again. I just can't."

Candler felt bad for the lady. She'd had a clear choice. She could make a payment on her bill here at the store or she could hold back a few dollars to pay a crew to gather that herd for her. She'd done the right thing by wanting to ship the cattle for sale to the trackside brokers instead of trying to sell them range delivery on a book count. But things were even tighter for her than Candler had realized.

It occurred to him to wonder if he and Norm and Eddie Mannet would ever see the wages she'd be owing to them in another few months. He had the thought and half a second later felt a rush of shame for thinking about himself like that. Mrs. Wolbrough had two little boys to worry about. She was doing her best. Would continue to do her best, he was sure.

If in the long run she couldn't pay off, well, the three of them still had food to eat and a dry place to sleep. Losing their pay to a widow lady's needs was better than losing it to a roulette wheel, and God knew he'd done that before.

Mannet and Norm surely had blown their wages a time or two in the past as well. When this job was done, all three of them would just ride on in search of the next one, with pay in their pockets or without.

Candler looked at the needles and thread, which Ebbersley was covering with the palm of his hand.

What in the world was the man thinking? Candler thought with a scowl. Was he worried Candler would grab the items and run?

Or was he maybe a little bit ashamed of himself for acting so hard with a widow woman.

"I'll still be wanting those," Candler said, inclining his head toward the purchases.

"Fine. No credit, though. I meant that."

"Yes, sir. Twenty-eight cents, you said?"

"That's right."

Candler reached into his pocket and pulled out the loose change he'd gotten after paying for his beer. He carefully counted out and laid down two dimes and two nickels. Ebbersley grunted and gave him his two cents change.

"I don't mean to be a hard-ass," the storekeeper said. "I really don't."

"I understand, sir." Candler was not sure that he did understand, but Ebbersley sounded sincere. Probably he really was sorry.

Ebbersley wrapped the thread and needles in brown paper and twisted the ends of the paper tube that formed around the spools. "Is there anything else I can do for you, friend?"

"No, sir. This is just fine, thank you."

Candler went out to his horse and tucked his purchases into his saddlebags, then looked up and down the street for a café where he could buy himself a meal with some meat in it for a change.

His mouth was watering at the thought of a juicy pork chop swimming in gravy, or chicken fried crisp and delicious like you could find down in Texas but probably not up this far north.

The more he thought about a platter piled heavy with meat, the faster he walked. He was practically running by the time he got to the café he'd spotted down the street.

✢ 23 ✢

EDDIE MANNET WAS still winning. Norm Shear was still drinking. And there was one more thing Candler needed before he headed back to the Ladder without them. He approached the barman, whose name was Tim.

"Excuse me. That girl back there. Is she the only one you have here?"

"At this hour she is, yeah. I got two others, but they won't wake up till the sun goes down. You'd think if they saw daylight they'd melt away or something. Like one of those whatchamacallit bloodsucking things."

"Vampires," Candler suggested.

"Yeah, them. Someday I expect to walk back to their cribs and find them laying in a coffin full of dirt. You want Monique there?"

"She's busy."

"The hell she is," Tim said. "She hasn't moved from that guy's side since he got here. Which I wouldn't mind so much except he hasn't bought her the first drink. Not one. She needs to get her fat ass moving." Tim raised his voice and barked, "Monique. Get over here."

The girl left the chair she'd pulled close to Eddie's elbow and came across the room with a broad smile on her face. There wasn't a lick of sincerity in it. Candler knew that. But she had a nice smile anyway. It made her dimples show. Candler liked dimples.

Eddie looked mildly annoyed. If he had chosen to object to losing his good luck piece, Candler would have relented and let the girl stay. After all, it's rude to interfere with anything a gambler thinks is contributing to his luck. But Eddie was silent, and anyway the girl seemed pleased enough. She didn't even lose her smile when she saw her customer.

"Take this gentleman around back and show him a nice time, Monique."

"Yes, sir."

To Candler he said, "You can pay here." He smiled and added, "Policy, you understand. Not that you would do such a thing, but some of the rowdier boys think they can pay their money and have their fun and then pound on the girls until they get their money back and maybe a little more besides. They aren't so likely to get into that sort of trouble if it's me they'd be bracing for the money."

"No offense taken," Candler said. He reached into his pocket. "Fifty cents be about right?"

"Just right," Tim said.

Monique took Candler's arm. Her smile became even wider, which Candler would have thought nigh impossible except that he saw it for himself. "I'm all yours, honey. All yours."

✛ 24 ✛

CANDLER YAWNED AND stretched, then pulled his boots on. He had come back to the Ladder early last night and got the best night's sleep he could remember in quite some time. Relaxation will do that for a man, he thought. And he'd been very nicely relaxed when he returned from town.

He yawned again and stood up. Eddie Mannet looked like he hadn't slept in a week. He too was getting dressed to go back to work.

Norm, on the other hand, was getting undressed. He had been just as late as Eddie coming back from town. Although they had returned separately. For him, though, this was bedtime. He would sleep through the day and resume his night herding duties after supper tonight.

"Know what I h-h-heard?" Norm asked.

"Can't you even talk like a regular person?" Eddie snapped irritably.

It occurred to Candler that Norm's stammering only seemed to happen when he'd been around strangers. Here on the Ladder, with just the few people Norm was comfortable with, he spoke normally. But now the hesitation in his speech was back.

"What did you hear, Norm?" Candler asked.

"I h-heard the r-railroad is building a sp-spur up this way."

"Aw, you hear that sort of rumor all the time. Doesn't matter where you go. Everybody thinks they're going to get a railroad line."

"N-no, really," Norm insisted. "The g-guy I heard it from is a suh-suh-surveyor."

"And he was talking to a dummy like you?" Mannet asked, his voice heavy with sarcasm.

"He was t-talking to some-somebody else. I over heard th-them."

"You aren't lying to us?" Mannet demanded.

Norm shook his head. "S'truth, I tell you. The g-guy wasn't b-bragging or nothing. He was just talking to his f-f-friend."

"I'll be damned," Eddie said. He was smiling, his expression distant in thought, as he buttoned his shirt.

Norm pulled his trousers off and tossed them on the floor, then crawled beneath his blanket and covered his head with it. His bare feet were sticking out from under the blanket at the other end of the bed.

"Aren't you going to breakfast?" Candler asked.

"No. I'm still full from l-last night."

"Suit yourself. You ready, Eddie?"

"A railroad, huh?" Eddie said happily.

"That stuff is just talk," Candler said.

"Maybe not." Mannet took his hat down from one of the pegs Candler had tapped into the front wall. "Maybe not."

Candler was thinking about hotcakes, not railroads, as they walked in the crisp early morning darkness over to the house, where Mrs. Wolbrough would have breakfast waiting for them.

✤ 25 ✤

"I WANT TO make a swing back up to the north again to-day," Mannet announced once they were saddled and had the kinks worked out of their horses.

"There's nothing up that way," Candler protested. "You know good and well those cows all drifted south last winter. It was a waste of time when we rode north before and it would be again."

"There's some spots we didn't look," Mannet said. "I want to check them."

"Fine, but let's wait until we have everything cleared down south. Every day the Ladder cows are allowed to wander free they're apt to get even further away than they are now."

"No, dammit, I said we're riding north today, and that's that," Mannet insisted.

Eddie looked peeved. Not that that was anything particularly new. Eddie seemed to be annoyed about one thing or
another much of the time.

The man was also beginning to take himself pretty seriously in his self-appointed role as ranch foreman, Candler
thought. Usually he didn't mind Eddie tossing orders
around, since about as often as not they were orders that
Candler had gently suggested to him.

But . . . spending time on another swing to the north
where they already knew there were no Ladder cattle?

Eddie was up to something. Candler had no idea what
that something might be. But he was sure there was a reason Eddie came up with this cockamamie idea.

It was no spur-of-the-moment notion either, Candler
saw now. This morning Eddie had saddled his best big-
circle horse, a tough and leggy brute that had a hard mouth
and a nasty disposition but could work the whole day and
hardly break a sweat. That was on the plus side of things.
The animal would also pound a man's kidneys to pulp just
to get it started in the morning, and Eddie usually avoided
riding it, giving the jughead more rest than it really ought
to have and favoring mounts that were easier to put into a
working frame of mind.

"Since we're gonna be riding and not herding today,
then I'd best switch my saddle," Candler said.

He more than half expected Eddie to bellyache about
the delay, but Eddie surprised him again by giving him an
absentminded nod and saying, "That's fine. Pick you one
with some wind."

Candler pulled his kak, hobbled the bay he'd intended to ride today and turned it loose. He took his rope off the saddle he'd draped over a fence rail and walked out away from the corral to find the grazing remuda and bring the brown in, it being the closest thing he had in his string to a circle horse.

✤ 26 ✤

THE BOY DONALD was holding the cows on the grass beside a seasonal stream just a mile or so north of the buildings. Candler half expected Eddie to invite the kid along. He really did seem to bask in the boy's idol worshiping of him. But no such invitation was forthcoming.

They did pause to say a few friendly words, and Eddie complimented the boy on the fine job he was doing. Which of course was a bunch of booshwah. The cattle were hock deep in good grass and weren't going anywhere. All Donny had to do was sit up high on his horse's back and watch to see if there were any really determined bunch quitters to turn back. Riding rings around a bunch of contented cattle was nothing. Containing a batch of spooked cows, of course, was something entirely differ-

ent. Fortunately no one was asking that of the inexperi-
enced boy.

Difficult job or not, kids don't usually have any more
confidence than they have experience, and it was a good
thing to try and build up Donny's view of himself as a
cowhand. Candler wouldn't have thought Eddie Mannet
would care enough to bother with something like that.
He'd pretty much thought that Eddie's regard lay entirely
with Eddie and that the boy was just a means by which Eddie could feed his own ego.

Maybe he'd misjudged the Ladder's sort-of foreman,
Candler conceded to himself. Maybe.

They headed northeast at an easy lope, reached what
they'd been told was Tomlinson Creek and followed it for a
spell, then turned west to a high bluff that lay at the base of
the hills that bordered the Ladder on that end.

It occurred to Candler that the course they were following was the same they'd been told should constitute the
Ladder's claimed home range.

That was made all the more clear when they followed
the imaginary boundary south well past the buildings,
turned east across the southern boundary line, then north
again along the road until they again reached Tomlinson
Creek and were back within three quarters of a mile from
where they'd started out that morning.

By then it was past time to head back in for supper, and
Candler's belly was growling. He wasn't used to missing
any meals these days, and quite frankly he did not want to
change that situation. Not in the slightest.

They did eventually get back. Norm was already out on night herd. They saw him from a distance but skirted wide around the bunch lest the presence of riders looming up out of the night put a scare into the cows and send them into a runaway.

Candler and Mannet stripped their saddles and hobbled the horses before turning them out to graze; then they carried their empty lunch pails and headed to the house to see if there was anything leftover from supper for them.

Not once during the day had they made so much as a token attempt to find strayed cows. All they'd done was to cover ground and look at what was around them.

"TOMORROW IS SUNDAY, you know," Eddie announced over the breakfast table a couple days later, breakfast consisting of corn cakes and some sort of tea that Mrs. Wolbrough brewed up from some of the weeds that grew round about. There was no sugar to help make the bitter stuff palatable, so they settled for the heavy and not entirely pleasant taste of molasses. And now even the molasses was running low.

"Is it?" the lady asked from the stove, where she was frying more of the corn dodgers, for the boys and herself. "I seem to have lost track."

The truth was that Candler had no idea what day of the week it was either. He hadn't bothered to inquire when they were in town. There was no reason to care. He had no appointments scheduled except with the top side of a horse and the back side of a cow, and neither one of them cared about the days either.

"Yes, ma'am, it surely is." Eddie smiled and took a sip of the awful tea and another bite of corn cake. "It occurs to me, ma'am, that you and the yonkers might care to attend services tomorrow."

"Church? Do you mean we should go in to church?"

"I do, ma'am. I believe it would do the both of you a world of good."

"Oh, I don't know, I . . ."

"What I was thinking, ma'am, was that I could hitch the wagon good and early, and after breakfast drive us all to town. We could go to church. That is, if you wouldn't mind being seen with a sinner such as myself. I can't speak for the crew. Haven't asked them would they care to attend. We could pack along a bucket of these fine corn dodgers you make and have those for our lunch, an' then come back in the afternoon once the preaching is done."

Mrs. Wolbrough's hand went to her hair and patted down some of the flyaway wisps that always ringed her head. Candler doubted she even knew she'd done it. It was that sort of perfectly automatic gesture that women seem to do.

After the hair she touched her throat. Candler suspected she was thinking about what to wear, how to turn herself out for the other ladies to see.

"I never thought . . . never considered . . ."

"Now, ma'am, I think it would be a right nice thing for you and those yonkers of yours to take in the Sunday services," Mannet persisted. "What d'you say? Shall I have the wagon here come breakfast tomorrow?"

"I don't know, I . . ."

"You don't have t' decide right now," Eddie magnanimously offered. "You can tell me tonight what you want to do."

But Eddie and Candler and probably even Norm too knew good and well what that decision would be. Candler could see it written clear in the softening of Mrs. Wolbrough's plain and usually strained features.

It seemed they would be going to church tomorrow.

At Eddie Mannet's suggestion.

Now there, Candler thought, was a true amazement. Damn if it wasn't.

✦ 28 ✦

EDDIE HAD THE wagon hitched and pulled around to the front door before the break of day. He'd even put the harness on himself. Candler hadn't known Eddie knew how to do all that common stuff; he usually delegated menial chores like that to Candler or to Norm Shear.

"Not me," Norm said when he was invited to go to church. "You go. I sleep."

But then of course he had just spent the night riding circles around a bunch of cows and singing to them. Not hymns though. The good folks in the church likely would not appreciate hearing any of Norm's made-up verses. Candler had heard some of them, and they just about made *him* blush.

Norm might not want to go to services, but that did not put a damper on his appetite. He joined the rest at breakfast, ate everything within reach and then mumbled something on his way back to the dugout.

"Will you be joining us, Mr. Chandler?" the lady asked.

"Yes, ma'am, I will."

"Very well. Would you please put this lunch basket in the wagon? And you might take this pail to Mr. Shear. We'll not be back in time to have lunch here."

"Yes, ma'am."

"Mr. Mannet, I must say that you are turned out quite grandly this morning."

Eddie smiled and preened a little. It was true though that he had taken some pains with his appearance this morning. His hair was slicked down with some sort of perfumed oil, and he was wearing a crisp new celluloid collar and string tie and a freshly brushed black suit coat, a pair of clean britches and boots that he'd stayed up last night to polish with soot and axle grease.

What he was not wearing was his guns. Of course they were going to church and all that, but Eddie liked to show off his guns and it surprised Candler that he was not wearing them for this trip into town now.

"Boys, finish your breakfast now. Hurry. We dasn't be late today."

Candler took the big picnic basket out to the wagon while Mrs. Wolbrough got her two boys wiped down and their shirttails tucked in. That would last for the first couple hundred yards of travel maybe, but at least they started out nice and tidy.

When the family came outside a few minutes later, Mrs. Wolbrough had changed into her good dress, which was made of a pale blue, shiny, silky-looking cloth and came complete with a big hat with a trailing ribbon that matched the material of the dress and a lacy little shawl that wouldn't do a thing to provide warmth but did look nice. She was even carrying a dainty parasol and a cloth hand-bag, both of them sort of an ivory color. Candler wouldn't have been surprised if this had been her wedding dress.

The way the dress hung loose at the shoulders and the waist showed she had lost a bunch of weight since the garment was new. She must have been positively plump back then. Back then.

The boys seemed excited to be going to town. James was running in circles making flapping motions with his arms. Could be he intended to fly there. Donny ran James down, boosted him into the back of the wagon and then crawled in beside him, while Eddie Mannet rather ceremoniously assisted Mrs. Wolbrough into the front, then ran around to unclip the horses from the hitching weights and drop the weights into the wagon bed.

Eddie climbed onto the seat and unwrapped the lines from the whip socket. By then Candler had gotten into the wagon bed with the boys, and they were all set.

"Come on, everyone, let's sing," Eddie called out as he put the team into motion. "We'll start with 'The Old Rugged Cross,' shall we? All together now . . ."

Eddie broke into loud song. Mrs. Wolbrough rather hesitantly joined him. The boys and John Candler sat in the back and marveled at it all.

Whoever would have thought that Eddie Mannet would know the words, Candler mused. But he did. Yessir, he surely did.

✦ 29 ✦

THE CHURCH WAS at the edge of town, at the opposite end from the establishments that did their business on the other six days—or nights—of the week. Candler had seen family chapels that were bigger.

Not, he supposed, that the Boss cared about the size of the building. When it came to that it surely was the size of the heart that counted.

Darn good thing too that it was not the size of the congregation that mattered either, for there were only three rigs parked outside when the Ladder arrived. Of course some folks walked over from the houses in town, and a few more wagons rolled in over the course of the morning.

When they first arrived, Eddie jumped down off the driving box and ran around to hand Mrs. Wolbrough down.

He offered his arm and escorted her inside. And the boys went helling off at a run to get under somebody else's feet.

That left Candler to lead the horses off to the side and take them out of the traces. He hobbled the horses and led them off a few rods to where there was a little grass they could crop, then went back to the wagon and slid the picnic basket under the seat so it wouldn't be in direct sun. Not that he expected there would be anything inside that was subject to spoiling.

Once the team was taken care of, he used his hat to pound off some of the dust that had billowed up off the wheels on the bumpy, bouncy drive in from the Ladder, and he was about as ready as he was likely to become.

It had been . . . it had been an awful long while since he was in any sort of church. The prospect of it now felt intimidating, so that there were flutters of nervousness in his belly. Ten thousand crazed horseflies on the loose in there.

Not that waiting around was going to make it any better. He took a deep breath and marched himself around to the front of the little church and up the steps.

At the front door he very carefully wiped his boots as clean as they were going to get, then stepped forward to accept the greeting from an elderly couple who were stationed there to offer handshakes and welcomes.

The man smiled and offered his hand.

Then Candler was through the portal and remembered at the last moment to reach up and snatch his hat off.

The lady of the pair took one look at John Candler's face and turned pale.

She straightened up a good two inches taller than she had been, and she gasped. She looked as if she might drop into a faint and her husband stepped forward to grasp her elbow and steady her.

When he did that, he shouldered Candler out of the way, forcing him back into the door frame. He was only trying to protect his wife. Candler knew that. Of course he did. But even so the man's broad back was a little hard to swallow.

There were times . . . there were times when Candler forgot how bad it looked to somebody who was seeing it for the first time.

"I'm sorry, I . . . I . . . Oh, shit." He spun around and jammed his hat back on as he fled down the church steps and across the short grass toward town.

✦ 30 ✦

THE SALOON DID not open until past noon on Sundays, Candler discovered, so he had to idle around like an out-of-work loafer for several hours. He could hear singing coming from the church; then later there was a babble of voices when services were over and the people streamed out, exchanging news and gossip, and in the case of the women very likely making catty comments about those who were not a part of the immediate conversation group. Candler was familiar enough with the way such things went.

Mrs. Wolbrough and the boys were among the last to leave the church. The lady stopped to have a brief conversation with the man who had been standing in the doorway shaking hands as everyone left. That of course would be the preacher.

Candler was sure he had seen the preacher in town before, although acting in some other role. Then he remembered. The fellow preached on Sunday mornings, but during the week he was the town barber. He'd given Candler a shave just a few days earlier on that day off.

Eddie Mannet, standing close by the Wolbrough family, said something to the preacher also and shook the man's hand. Then Eddie took Mrs. Wolbrough by the elbow and guided her away from the wagon and on toward town.

Candler was fairly sure Eddie saw him sitting on a bench in the shade before the hardware, which was closed for Sunday. Eddie did not acknowledge Candler. He led the Wolbroughs to the café and held the door for them, then followed them inside.

Candler was not close enough to overhear what was being said, but it was obvious from facial expression and body language that Mrs. Wolbrough was protesting the extravagance while at the same time enjoying the prospect of having a meal that was prepared and served by someone other than herself.

The boys looked like going out to eat was to be a major treat.

For that matter it probably was. They might have been able to manage café meals when their father was still alive but certainly not since then.

It was also obvious that Eddie had no intention of spending any of his gambling winnings on John Candler.

That was fair enough; Candler had no desire to be beholden to the man. The truth was that he did not care for

Eddie overmuch. For damn sure he was not going to kow-
tow to him.

Tim the bartender—Candler did not know his last
name—appeared from a direction that suggested he was
not himself a churchgoer and unlocked the saloon.

Candler rose, his joints protesting a little too much for
comfort, and walked over to become one of the saloon's
first customers of the day. He still had enough in his pocket
to buy a beer and a trip to the free lunch platter.

After that he figured he could break out the corn
dodgers in that picnic basket and wait there at the wagon
for Eddie and his guests to finish enjoying their day in
town.

✢ 31 ✢

THE NIGHTMARE RETURNED that night. He hadn't
had it in . . . How long had it been, anyway? Since
before he came to the Ladder. He was sure about that.

He woke up trembling and drenched in cold sweat.

The dream was not always identical in the particulars,
but it was always very much the same sort of thing.

He was running through a plowed field.

He held something in his hand. Sometimes it was a
sword, sometimes a staff, once in a great while a rifle.

He could not see anything any distance away. Everything around him was hazy. He knew that was because the
field was wreathed in smoke. He knew it was smoke even
though he could not smell it.

In his dreams he could see but could not hear or smell
anything.

He waved the object overhead, motioning behind him as if to exhort the others to follow.

The others. He knew they were there. He could not see them in the smoke but he knew they were there. Following. Faithful even unto death.

Something, some great and horrid creature loomed dark and menacing in front of him.

Flame burst in his face. He knew it was fire. Knew it burned his flesh. But he could not feel the burning or smell the peculiar stench of live flesh being roasted; nor could he feel the impact that he knew would attend the flame.

And then he woke.

At that point he always woke up. Shaking. Sweating. Frightened.

The dream. He knew it would never leave him. Not for as long as he still drew breath.

But, oh, he so very much enjoyed the nights of respite between those nightmares.

Candler drew his blanket up to his chin and lay awake, staring sightlessly toward the ceiling. He would not go back to sleep. Not this night.

✦ 32 ✦

IN THE MORNING Candler's eyes burned from lack of sleep, and his mouth was foul. He was afraid this was going to be a very long day.

He took some of the bad taste out of his mouth with a dab of salt clinging to a wet finger which he used to clean his teeth. And the fatigue was reduced even if not eliminated when he went inside for breakfast and smelled the wonderfully welcome aroma of freshly boiled coffee.

There was coffee for each of them *and* a can of milk *and* a bowl of sugar—not molasses, sugar; real, white crystal sugar—to go along with the usual hotcakes.

Those additions pretty much explained what had been in the bundle Eddie Mannet carried back to the wagon yesterday afternoon and then took inside the house when they returned to the Ladder. He'd bought some luxuries for them all to share. Had to have gotten them with his poker winnings from when they were all in town a few days earlier.

That was damn nice of Eddie. Mighty unexpected too. Candler hadn't thought Eddie the sort who would think to do something like that for a widow woman, especially for one who owed him money.

Candler was not so surprised that he intended to look this particular gift horse in the mouth, however. He sat down and with great pleasure filled his cup with steaming coffee and laced the heady brew with milk and sugar. There was nothing like a good cup of coffee to get a day started.

He let his plate of hotcakes get cold while he sat there slowly sipping at the coffee, ate the flannel cakes and then topped the meal off with another cup of that marvelous coffee.

He felt pretty decent when he picked up his lunch pail and went outside after that. Decent enough that he should be able to get through the day just fine, in fact.

"Eddie," he said as they were saddling their mounts for the day.

"Yeah, whadda you want?"

"Thanks," Candler said.

Eddie looked surprised. He blinked a few times. Then scowled and ducked his head, giving his concentration to making sure his cinch was pulled just tight enough.

Candler was really beginning to think he'd been misjudging Eddie all this time. It could be that a man for all his bluster and flamboyance was shy at heart.

That train of thought did not last past Candler's butt hitting the leather of his saddle seat. The roan he'd chosen for the day gave a snort and a squeal, dropped its head and began to fight against the prospect of hard work, and Candler no longer had time to think of anything but remaining on top until the dang horse got it through its head that it was not going to be the boss here.

✦ 33 ✦

They rode hard for the next five days but accomplished little. There were still Ladder cows roaming loose, but few of them were close enough to be found on a one-day sweep away from the house. Even starting south two hours before daybreak, by the time they got down to where the cattle were it was just about time to turn around and start back again.

Mannet brought it up on Saturday evening as they were pulling their saddles and hobbling the horses ready to go back out onto the grass. "Next week we're gonna have to take the wagon and stay down there for a spell."

Candler had been thinking the same thing for the past several days but had said nothing about it.

Now that the subject was on the table, he did say, "There's some rough country down there. D'you think we should take a pack horse instead? Lord knows we don't have much to carry, and a horse travels easier than a wagon in country like that."

"We'll take the wagon," Eddie said firmly.

Candler shrugged and turned away. It wasn't worth arguing about.

Sunday morning Eddie once again loaded the Wolbrough family into the wagon and drove to town, this time with Norm Shear riding along, although whether the big man wanted to attend services or simply get a break in town Candler did not know.

He himself chose to stay at the ranch rather than be packed into a small building with a bunch of strangers. That one experience at the church door had been quite enough. He did not want to repeat it.

"Are you sure you'll not come with us, Mr. Chandler?"

He took his hat off and stared at his boots, turning his head to the side a little so the disfigurement was not so easily seen. "No, ma'am, I'll just laze around here. Get some sleep. You know. Like that."

"As you wish then, but you know you are welcome."

"Yes, ma'am." He knew no such thing but was not going to tell that to Mrs. Wolbrough.

Eddie checked to see that the boys and Norm were settled, then shook out the lines and took them off toward town.

Candler wandered back to the dugout, but he knew good and well he would not be taking any naps. The habits of work were strong, and he would have felt like he was cheating if he slept the daylight away. Not that he knew who it was he would be cheating exactly. The day was his own. Even so, it just would not have felt right to him.

He fetched the bow saw along with the maul and some wedges and spent a couple hours reducing the woodpile into stove-lengths that were cut, split and stacked—Mrs. Wolbrough would need a supply of those while he and Eddie were away to the south—and walking around the corral checking to see that the posts were solidly set and the rails reasonably tight. It amazed him sometimes how a fence could take a notion to fall apart the moment a man turned his back and quit paying attention.

He took the little horse that Donny usually used and rode out to find the steeldust that was in his string. He intended to take the steeldust in the morning and wanted time to look it over now, feel of its muscles and look over its feet in good light to assure himself there were no stone bruises or muscle pulls that he needed to worry about.

If they needed spare horses while they were away down south, they would have to make the wagon team do double duty, but hopefully there would be no need for that.

Candler raided Mrs. Wolbrough's kitchen for some cornmeal, lard and salt and made himself a lunch of stick bread that he baked inside the stove in the dugout.

Then he treated himself to the luxury of a bath. With the lady off the premises he was able to strip down and immerse himself in the trough, lying back and soaking some of the sweat and dust off the outside and some of the aches and pains out of the middle of his battered body. Old scars stood out prominently in the harsh light of afternoon, although Candler himself no longer thought anything about them.

He lifted his face to the warmth of the sun and closed his eyes for a few moments while the cool water cleansed and refreshed him. It was as close to self-indulgent laziness as he knew how to come.

✦ 34 ✦

I T WAS EASY for Eddie to say they would take the wagon. He wasn't driving the damn thing.

Eddie led the way on horseback, riding the jug-headed brown he'd chosen for the gather down south and leading Candler's steeldust. Candler, on the other hand, had to figure out a path for the wagon.

A man astride can cross pretty much any gully or washout. Take the horse down sliding on its butt if necessary. But a wagon needs a gentle incline, or at the very least one that won't topple things and cause a wreck.

A wagon is a heck of a lot wider than the single track a horse uses too, so it can be close to impossible to force a wagon through a stand of aspen, for instance, or through spreading juniper or thick scrub oak. A rock that a horse would step over without hardly noticing can completely block a wagon wheel. Or shatter one if the driver is not careful.

The worst thing was that Eddie's pathfinding abilities made scant allowance for the wagon's limitations. Candler spent pretty much the entire day grumbling and mumbling and cussing Eddie Mannet under his breath.

They rolled south by southeast for the whole day, then found a place to set up camp where there was good grass for the animals on a broad flat above what once had been a beaver pond but was now silted over. A bare strip of red gravel eight or ten yards wide meandered down the middle of the flat, with a trickle of water flowing in the middle. The seasonal flow was a half inch or so deep now. Later on in the summer it would disappear altogether, and then it would emerge again in the spring, fed by the melt runoff from next winter's snows.

Candler dug a sump in the gravel bed that when it filled would be deep enough to dip water out of for their own use and to serve as a sort of water trough for the horses as well. The cattle, when they gathered some, would just have to make out the best they could.

A couple old stone fire rings showed that others before them had thought the spot a good one, and on the hillside above the grass flat there were some larger circles of rock left behind by Indians who'd used them to hold down the edges of their tipis.

"Look at that, Candler. How old d'you suppose those tent rings are?"

He shrugged. "Hundred years maybe. Two hundred. Could be older."

"You think so?"

"Yes. It looks to me like they were put here when there was a pond in the place where now it's all grass and solid ground. Otherwise you'd think they would be down close to where the water is."

"That's all right then," Mannet said. "But if any of those red sons of bitches comes around, I'll show them who's boss these days."

"Eddie, there hasn't been any Indian trouble around here for years."

"Even so. Say, you got that dough ready to bake? I'm getting hungry."

"It'll only be a minute. Let's make something clear though. I'm not your cook and I'm not your hey-boy. I'm cooking today. Tomorrow it's your turn," Candler told him. He meant it too. If Eddie didn't want to share the camp chores, Candler was perfectly willing to fend for himself, strictly himself alone, and let Eddie do the same for whatever he wanted done.

Mannet looked like he might want to get prickly about it, then he let go of the resentment and nodded. He was not Candler's boss after all, he only acted like he was, and until or unless Mrs. Wolbrough named him Ladder's foreman he was only another hand who liked to be bossy.

"Do you want to spend a day building a holding pen or should we just loose graze them on the flat here?" Candler asked, figuring it would soothe Eddie's feelings some to have Candler defer to him now with the question.

"We'd best make a pen," Eddie said. "I don't want to catch 'em just to see them sneak away again overnight."

Candler nodded. "I agree. Tell you what. Tomorrow before we get to cutting trees, let's take a look around. Could be there's other outfits have done the same. It's a lot easier to repair a holding pen than to build one fresh."

"Right. First thing in the morning," Mannet said.

Candler finished making the thick, sticky dough that he had been working on and handed half of it and a greenwood stick to Eddie.

"Jesus, Candler, I hope you washed before you kneaded this. You've got flour up to your elbows and dough stuck all over your hands."

Candler held his hands up and examined them, turning them one way and then another. "Can't remember if I did or not, but they look pretty clean now. If you run into anything that crunches, though, I'd recommend you not look at it too close. You might not like what the little black bits are."

Mannet laughed and began packing some of the dough around a dingle stick so he could bake it over their campfire.

✢ 35 ✢

CANDLER FELT GOOD. He liked working out away
from people, out in empty country with a horse and
some cows and a job to do. He didn't even mind doing
work that had to be done afoot, although he'd known a fair
number of fellows—good hands who were proud of their
knowledge and abilities—who would draw their time and
leave a job if they were told to work with an ax or a shovel.
Candler just did whatever work was needed. And he long
ago got over pride and the posturing that goes with it. He
had exchanged a different sort of satisfaction for it and
learned to take pleasure in completing whatever job might
come his way. He didn't always do the best job. He knew
that. But he always gave it his level best, and perhaps there
was something to be said for that.

At the moment he was concerned with getting a cow pen built.

There were no old pens in the vicinity that they might rebuild, so they had to make one.

Eddie found a couple blowdowns that would provide a good bit of their building material. Candler worked on the ground with saw and ax to cut the fallen trees into manageable size while Eddie used the team of horses and a chain to drag the gray, weathered trunks into place. Pile enough of them in a line, limbs still attached, and they would form a hedge-like fence of tangled wood good enough to contain a bunch of beeves for a few days.

"Let's stop for dinner," Eddie said when they'd gathered perhaps a quarter of what they needed. "I'm about tuckered."

Candler took his hat off and ran the back of his wrist over his forehead to wipe the sweat away. His expression was unchanged, but he was amused by Eddie's worries about overwork. Candler was the one who was sodden with sweat. All Eddie had to do was guide the team while the horses did the dragging.

Still, the thought of coffee and a bite of something in his belly wasn't bad. "Fine by me." He gathered up his tools and placed them in the bed of the parked wagon, then helped Eddie remove the harness from the pulling horses and hobble them so they could graze for their dinner while the men took theirs.

Eddie had ridden to the blowdown and headed back to

their camp at a lope. Candler, having driven the wagon there, had to walk. He knew better than to expect Eddie to give him a ride two-up on the brown.

By the time he got there, Eddie had the fire built up out of the morning's coals and had water on to boil for coffee. Apparently he believed Candler's warning from the day before, for he was busy preparing dough for the stick bread that would be their lunch.

"When I'm done here," Eddie said, "an' the fire dies down a bit, I'll put some beans on the coals. Let 'em stew slow and they oughta be just about right by the time we're ready for supper."

"Sounds good."

"This afternoon I might see can I find us some meat too," Eddie said. "A man gets tired of nothing but beans and cornpone."

"Range venison?" Candler asked.

"Uh huh. Likely." Range venison was the variety that came wearing a beef hide to start with but became venison once the hide was removed.

Candler offered no objection. He knew it would do no good if he did. And anyway he would enjoy having some meat in their diet too.

There were some ranchers nowadays who objected to cowhands taking meat out of the herd, although back when beeves were cheap and plentiful that was regarded as a normal perquisite of the job.

Eating range venison was one of those instances in which Candler preferred the old ways to the new.

Candler went to cut some fresh dingle sticks, and when Eddie was done with his mixing, Candler exchanged one of them for half of the raw dough. He looked at the bland dough and thought about red meat, and his mouth began to water.

"Beans and venison sounds pretty good," he said.

"Yeah," Mannet agreed. "Don't it just."

The two hunkered down on opposite sides of the fire to hold the dough over the coals for baking.

The aroma of boiling coffee surrounded them. The sky was clear and intensely blue. A hawk or maybe it was an eagle made lazy circles high above the earth. Life, Candler reflected, wasn't entirely bad.

✢ 36 ✢

IT TOOK THREE days, not one, to complete the holding pen, mostly because Eddie Mannet kept finding things he had to do other than cutting brush and blowdown and dragging it into place. Particularly after lunch he would disappear, generally carrying a box of .45 ammunition with him, and shortly there would be the repeated boom of pistol shots. Target practice, Candler assumed, or more work on Eddie's fast draw.

Not that Candler minded being left alone like that. He was comfortable with only himself for company and enjoyed having the work to do. It was not all that important what the work was or how long it would take to complete. Whatever the task, he would give it his best.

And he did enjoy the four large chunks of range venison

that Eddie's six-guns provided. Not all of those gunshots had been fired just for practice.

Eddie kept a straight face when he referred to the meat as venison. But you don't ride up on a mulie or a whitetail either one and put a bullet into it at pistol range, and they did not have a rifle in the camp.

Even so, the meat was tasty and Candler was pleased to have it. They sliced the first roast into steaks and cooked those right away. The three remaining pieces were wrapped tight in Candler's slicker and sunk at the bottom of the sump they'd dug into the creek bed. The meat would stay cool there and should last for a week or longer without turning color and becoming slimy. And it certainly couldn't be found by the blowflies when it was submerged in the chill creek water.

"Tomorrow we'll start bringing the Ladder cows in," Eddie said over the coals of their campfire the night the pen was completed. "I have a bunch of them spotted already. It won't be any trouble to bring them together."

"How many do you think you can handle with just you driving them?"

"Just me?"

"One of us has to drive the wagon, you know. That leaves the other to push the cows. You want to drive the wagon back and leave me on the cows instead?"

"No," Eddie said quickly. "No." He tossed a pebble into what was left of the fire. "I hadn't thought about that."

Candler said nothing. But Eddie certainly should have

thought of it before he insisted they bring the wagon. Their supplies and the few tools could easily have been carried on a pack horse and the pack animal herded home right along with the gather of beeves. That would have allowed both of them to do the droving, and two can handle moving cattle four or five times easier than one man and horse can.

"How long d'you figure to stay here?" Candler asked.

"I dunno. Till we get a hundred head together maybe. It depends on how many Ladders we find down here. Do you recall the woman ever saying how many cows that husband of hers was running?"

Candler shook his head. "If she said, I don't recollect it."

Mannet felt of his chin and stared off into the evening sky. "I wonder how many of them there are."

Candler shrugged. "Couple hundred would be my guess. Not much bigger, I wouldn't think, or the guy would've left his widow better fixed than she is."

"This range, what with all the water that's available, I'd think an outfit like the Ladder could handle four, even five hundred head."

"Sure. If a man had that many. Which I'd say Wolbrough didn't."

"But if a man started with what Wolbrough did have, he could build up to five hundred head in no time, wouldn't you think?"

"Yes. If he was careful of his increase. Sold off as little as he could get by with. Rode hard during the winter to make sure he didn't lose much to the wolves and the cold, and watched in spring to keep the bears and eagles from taking his calves, and got down to help with the birthings whenever he was needed. Yes, he could build his herd on a place with good grass and water like this country has."

"And if he didn't get himself blind drunk and freeze his own self to death," Mannet added.

"That's only a rumor."

"I heard it for fact last Sunday. Fella said it straight out. Wolbrough got hisself soused and fell off into a snowbank."

"Say it in front of the widow, did he?"

"You know better'n that. But he said it just the same."

"Pity," Candler said, but it was only spoken out of respect for Mrs. Wolbrough. He hadn't known her husband and felt no particular sympathy for him now. This was a hard country and a harder life, and no one had forced Wolbrough into it.

Instead of agreeing, Eddie Mannet chuckled a little, as if something funny had been said. He grinned and stood, snapped a twig between his fingers and tossed it onto the dying coals. The twig flared up, sending a flush of light all around and quickly dying as the dry wood was soon consumed.

"Maybe not such a pity," Mannet said.

"What's that?"

"Nothing. Nothing at all." Eddie turned and walked off into the gathering dark.

✦ 37 ✦

"WE WON'T TRY to brand any of these calves," Eddie said later in the week. "Not down here we won't. I figure we're better off to take them back and do all the branding at once, up there where we'll have Shear and the kid to help out. A man Shear's size, he can do the mugging. The kid can hold the herd. I'll cut the calves away from the mama cows, and that leaves you to handle the fire and the iron."

"You've been thinking about this," Candler said.

"Just common sense," Eddie told him.

They were seated close to the supper fire, their bellies warm and full of roast venison, cornpone and coffee. The coffee supply was down to almost nothing, but there was always something that a man could brew a tea out of if nothing else. Juniper or rose hips or some dang thing. Over the years Candler had drunk just about everything short of horse piss. And come to think of it, there'd been some bar whiskies that might have included that too.

"We have . . . what? Sixty-five cows, eight steers and thirteen calves now," Candler observed.

"What's your point?"

"I think it's about time we start them back."

"We'll give it a couple more days," Mannet insisted.

"Ladders are getting kinda thin on the ground around here," Candler said. "Could be we'd do better to take these back and come down another time to pick up anything we've missed. You know. Set up a camp a little ways east from here maybe. I think we've got just about all the Ladder beeves we're going to find right close around here." Candler smiled. "Besides, we're about out of venison."

Eddie grunted and reached for the coffee can. "Yeah, we could use more supplies anyhow. I guess we could come back again after we've got this bunch settled where they belong. But I like it here. We got the pen all finished and everything. Be a pity to have to make another one."

"Better to build another pen than to waste time looking for Ladders where there aren't any," Candler said. "All we're seeing now is CTs and Double Crosses."

"Yeah, that's so. All right then. We'll leave first light tomorrow." He stood and dusted off the seat of his britches.

Candler nodded and poured the last of the coffee into the tin can he used as a cup. The brew was thick with grounds and had a sharply bitter flavor, but it was hot. And he'd sure had worse.

✦ 38 ✦

THE TRIP THAT had taken a day coming down took two and a half going back, not only because the cattle slowed them down but also because Eddie Mannet spent half of the last afternoon making more "venison." He drove a steer off far enough from the rest of the bunch that the sound of a gunshot wouldn't spook the whole herd, then knocked the steer down with a bullet behind its ear.

Once the steer was down, Mannet returned to watching the herd and told Candler to butcher the steer and load it into the wagon. Candler got the idea that was why Mannet had insisted they bring the wagon in the first place, although he couldn't put his finger on any particular reason why he thought that.

"And mind you save the hide," Mannet cautioned. "A green hide ought should be worth a dollar or maybe more."

Candler wondered who Eddie's hey-boy was last year.
But he said nothing. And Mannet was right about one thing
anyway. The hide would be worth a good dollar in town,
and Mrs. Wolbrough could surely use the money.

Of course she could have used even more the twenty-
eight to thirty dollars a live steer would have brought her.
But this steer was dead now, and letting it go to waste
wouldn't do any of them any good.

He drove over to where the steer lay sprawled awkwardly on the hard soil, its neck twisted at an impossible
angle and a sightless glaze filming its eyes.

A swarm of bluebottle flies was already gathering to
feast on the blood. Leave the carcass here for a week where
the coyotes and the magpies, the wolves and the buzzards,
the mice and the foxes and the ants and such could get at it
and there would be nothing left but bone and some scraps
of hide. Leave it a little longer and there would be only the
bones bleaching in the sun.

That was the way of things though. Anything living was
destined to be food for something else. Anything and
everything, people included. Although of course no one
ever liked to think of themselves as someday being worm
food.

They would be though. There was no getting around it.

Candler sat on the seat of the wagon and chided himself
for becoming so damned melancholy. It was only a steer he
had to deal with here. It was only meat.

It was just that he'd seen so much. So awful much.

He sighed and climbed down from the driving box and

reached under the seat for the whetstone—he would have to sharpen his knife a couple times before he was done here, he knew—and while he was at it, he got the ax out too. There's nothing like an ax for quickening up the task of butchering a large critter.

✢ 39 ✢

M RS. WOLBROUGH WAS overwhelmed with the idea of having so much fresh meat in her larder.

"The thing is," Eddie explained, just as sincere as he knew how, "the poor animal stepped in a badger hole, ma'am, and broke its leg. Isn't that right, Candler? Didn't it break its leg? The left fore if I remember a'right."

Candler said nothing, did not even lend a grunt to the conversation lest that be taken as affirmation of Eddie's lies. There was nothing that could be said, after all. Nothing that would serve any purpose.

"Can't fix a broke leg, ma'am, so we did the next best thing we could and put the poor thing outa its misery. And I knew you wouldn't want good meat to go to waste, so we brung it on in with us."

"So much," she said. "There is so much of it. It . . . Really it is quite wonderful. And I know you had no choice. Thank you for being so considerate."

"That's our pleasure, ma'am," Eddie said, hat in hand and warm smile on his face.

No wonder the man was so good at poker, Candler thought. There wasn't a true feeling that could be found on his surface. Besides, he probably cheated. Certainly he would if he thought he could get away with it. And Candler suspected that Eddie was one of those people who pretty much thought he could get away with whatever he wanted.

They ate well that night. Good range beef fried in tallow, and corn bread to go with it. And for dessert there was a special treat. Mrs. Wolbrough somewhere had learned to swirl molasses into the hot beef tallow when she was done with the cooking and serve that up as a sweet. Any man who ever went droving on the far trails knew the pleasure of tallow and 'lasses. Now the Wolbrough boys did too, the both of them licking it up like it was better than candy.

"D'you know anything about branding, son?" Mannet asked Donny once the eating was done and night had settled over the place.

"No, sir. I've heard it's exciting. Will you teach me?"

Eddie tousled the boy's hair and patted his shoulder. "Tomorrow," he said. "Tomorrow we're gonna brand the calves we brought back today. And then . . . Say now, I just had a thought. Candler and me, we're gonna ride back down south an' gather in some more of your cows. Could be your mama will let you ride along with us. Camp out under the stars an' drink black coffee." He laughed. "We'll teach you to smoke and chew and spit. Well, I expect you already know how to spit."

"Mr. Mannet! Please!"

"Oh, I'm just funning the boy, ma'am," Eddie said with a grin and a chuckle. "But I'd wager he would benefit from the experience. He's already doing a man's job. Ought to be he gets to enjoy a few of a man's pleasures too. Like being out in God's own country with a good horse an' work to do. What do you say? Can he come with us when we go south again? I mean, if he wants to, that is."

"I want to, Mama. Please? *Please?*"

She began collecting the plates off the dinner table. "Maybe. Mind now, Donald Lewis Wolbrough, I am not saying you can. Only that I will think about it."

The boy laughed and looked at his idol. "She talks tough, you know, but she really means that I can go."

"We won't be going anyplace for a few days," Eddie said, "but tomorrow you and me will sit down and start making up your bedroll and warbag. They're part of a top hand's tools, you might say. We'll do that then."

Eddie looked up at Mrs. Wolbrough, who was drawing hot water from the reservoir built onto the side of her cooking range. "And I've kind of lost track of the days, ma'am. Perhaps you could remind us of what day of the week this is so we can drive in to church again. If you're of a mind to, that is."

"Yes, I would very much like that, Mr. Mannet. And this is Friday."

"Very good, ma'am. I'll look forward to that."

Candler stood and reached for his hat. Eddie was certainly acting like the perfect foreman here, wasn't he.

Well, that was to the lady's advantage. And doing for her, after all, was what they were being paid for here.

✢ 40 ✢

CANDLER DAMN NEAR wiped out the woodpile, loading almost everything into the wagon early on Saturday morning.

"Leave some for the rest of us, won't you," Eddie Mannet
complained.

"Have you ever tried to heat irons in an aspen wood
fire? Stuff burns fast and won't make coals worth spit. But
it's what we have. Besides, if there's any leftover I'll bring
it back. Figure we're better off to have too much on hand
than too little." He stopped what he was doing and took a
moment to wipe sweat out of his eyes. "What d'you care
anyhow? I'm the one doing all the work."

Mannet scowled and went stalking off to oversee something else.

Candler finished loading the wagon and told Mannet, "I

have the irons. Brought the ax and saw too. If we finish early enough, I'll stop on the way back and pick up some more wood. I thought I'd build my fire on that flat above the coulee where those two cow skulls are. You remember the place?"

"Course I remember."

"All right then. I figure that's as good a spot as any and better than most, and the ground is just about bare. Shouldn't be any danger of starting more fire than we want to see."

"All right, go ahead then. I'll go out an' help the kid drive the cows over there just before noon. That will give you plenty of time to get whatever coals you can and get the irons hot. Give Norm time enough to get a little sleep too. I'll ask the lady to shake him out at lunchtime, then he can come join us for the branding."

"Good enough." Candler shook the lines a little to get the team's attention and set off toward the spot he liked for the branding. He was in a pretty good mood. He liked being off by himself like this with work to do and no one around to bother him.

It was a good hour past sunrise by the time he reached the spot he wanted. He parked the wagon where it would be close by but shouldn't get in the way, then unhitched and hobbled the horses so they could graze until they were needed again.

He found a few reasonably flat rocks and arranged them on the ground. He did not need a fire ring, but he did want a good surface where he could lay the irons so they would

rest nicely in the coals. When he had coals for them. Then
he set about laying and lighting the fire. He would want it
to burn for an hour or so before he could even start heating
the branding irons, which had to be the just-right temperature if the brand was to be okay.

Too little heat and all you'd do was singe the hair without producing the permanent scarring that made a lasting,
readable brand. Too much and you'd end up with a
wound—an open invitation to screwworms and infection—
instead of a proper brand.

The heat of the iron had to be right, and the man applying it had to know how hard to press it onto the calf's hide
and how long to hold it there. It wasn't a skill that was all
that difficult to learn. But it was something that did have to
be learned, and in truth not everyone had the knack.

Candler whistled while he busied around until he got
things started. Then he stretched out underneath the wagon
so he could enjoy its shade and not have to worry about being stepped on by the horses, which were more interested
in investigating the contents of the wagon at the moment
than they were in eating the short, sparse grass up here.

He used his hat for a pillow and got a few winks in.

It was hard work, this branding.

Candler smiled a little while he dozed.

✦ 41 ✦

"THAT'S RIGHT, SON. Bring him on. Little closer. Little closer. Whoa!"

The boy was practically glowing with pride when he reined his horse to a halt, the bitter end of his catch rope dallied around the horn and a wildly protesting calf at the business end. Eddie seemed to have encouraged Donny to do more than just stay back holding the cows in a bunch. And that was good. The experience would be good for the kid, Candler figured, even if his mama took him back east to where he'd never see a cow again in his life. Just knowing he could do it, could rope a calf and bring it to the fire, the knowledge that he could do a man's job, would stay with him. It was something every boy needs if he is going to become a man someday, and this right now would stand Donny Wolbrough in good stead his whole life through.

Candler wondered if Eddie knew that and was deliberately doing something nice for the boy that Donny himself would not realize. Not for years. Maybe not forever. But it would be there. And maybe Eddie knew that.

Then again, Candler thought with a small smile, maybe Eddie just happened to blunder into a deed that was a better one than he'd intended it to be.

Candler checked to make sure he had a fresh iron ready. Norm walked down the rope to capture the skittish calf and half pick it up so he could throw the rope off and nod for the boy to go back to the bunch for another.

Donny seemed to be fascinated by the goings-on and sat where he was, watching while Norm dumped the calf onto its side and held it down.

Candler took an iron and applied it to the little animal's flank. The calf bawled and tried to kick itself free. Norm held it in place while Candler used the straight iron to make the three vertical parallel marks of the Ladder brand. He had to go back to the fire for a second iron to finish off with the cap and bottom strikes.

The brand Wolbrough had chosen was not all that big but it took a lot of burning to put it all on with only the running iron. It would have been much better if the man had paid a smith to make him a proper branding iron so the whole thing could be applied with one strike and be done with it. Get a uniform brand every time, be easier on the hand doing the branding and be less stress on the calf too.

But then maybe that was something Wolbrough intended to do but died before he got around to.

Donny watched throughout, not flinching away at the sight or seemingly bothered by the stink of the burning hair or the runny cow shit that squirted and sprayed all over when the calf reacted to the feel of the iron on its hide. By the end of the day Norm would be caked heavy with dirt and dust and dried crap, and Candler would be almost as filthy from working on the ground.

Eddie and the boy would only be layered with the dust that was as inevitable at a branding as was the sound of bawling cattle and the sizzle of burning hair.

Candler stuck the iron back into the coals, and Norm turned the calf loose to scramble onto its feet, shake itself off and scamper back in search of its mama.

"You can go back and get another one now, Donny," Candler said.

"What? Oh." He grinned. "Did I do that right, mister? Did I do good?"

"You did good, son. Now go get us another."

"Yes, sir."

Donny reined his horse away from the fire and headed back toward the little herd.

It would take a few minutes for Eddie to bring a calf out of the bunch to where Donny could put a loop over it, which meant that Candler and Norm could take themselves a little break.

Candler took his hat off and wiped the sweat from his forehead and out of his eyes. Norm went over to the wagon, to where they had a jug of drinking water. He rinsed his mouth and spat out the first dipper, drank some of the second and poured the rest over his head. Mugging was the hardest part of the branding, and Norm would be dead tired by the time they were done.

It was a good thing tomorrow was Sunday, so they would all be able to get a little rest.

"Here he comes with another one," Candler said after a bit. He went back to the fire and again checked the irons, picked one up and used a wire brush to clean some accumulated ash and hair and junk off the hot end, then tucked it back into the coals.

Hot day, he thought. And dusty. But they were getting it done. That was the important thing. They were getting the job done.

✢ 42 ✢

"Y OU WANTED TO see us, ma'am?" Candler asked, his hat off as respect required but held beside his head so it would cover the discoloration that consumed his face.

"Will you be coming to church with us this morning, Mr. Chandler?"

"No, ma'am, I don't expect so."

"Me neither," Norm said.

Eddie said nothing, but then it could be taken for granted that he would be driving the family to church, as had become his habit.

"Very well. That is your choice. I do want to remind you that this is the end of the month. You are each entitled to the remainder of your cash payment—five dollars, less the two you each were advanced." She opened a crocheted handbag and removed a silk snap purse, opened that and removed a handful of coins.

Very carefully she counted out a tiny two dollar and fifty cent quarter eagle for each of them, the minuscule coins smaller than dimes but beautiful, with a proud seated eagle on one side and an Indian head on the other. She added a half dollar into each hand and smiled, pleased with herself, as she snapped the purse shut again.

Payday was normally on a Saturday so the boys could raise a little hell with their money, but Mrs. Wolbrough probably did not know that. Candler smiled. Or maybe she did and this Sunday morning pay simply reflected her disapproval of raucous behavior.

As it was, Candler thought about riding into town for the day. There were some things he wanted to buy. A razor of his own would be nice since the Ladder did not offer one to share around. He was getting tired of using his knife blade. No matter how he tried, there was just no way you could make the thick blade of a knife match the sharpness of a proper razor.

The traditional pleasures beckoned too, a drink of whiskey and the soft warmth of a woman, even if it was a Sunday morning.

But he was still tired and he wanted to bathe again. He'd washed off the previous evening, but he had come to look forward to the luxury of a neck-deep soak on these Sunday mornings when there was no lady present and he could strip down without risking giving offense.

"C'n I ride along?" Norm asked. "I ain't goin' to church though."

"Certainly you may, Mr. Shear. Mr. Chandler, will you change your mind as well?"

"Thank you, ma'am, but no. I'll stay back if you don't mind."

"Then I shall set something in the warming oven for your dinner," she said.

"You're very kind, ma'am, thanks."

Candler got the team ready while Eddie was busy slicking his hair down and Norm was changing into some clothes that were a little cleaner than what he'd put on to start with. Norm was not big on doing laundry. Not that Candler particularly liked washing clothes either, but it was something that had to be done from time to time if a body didn't have the money to hire it done.

The rest of them drove off into the pink glow of the coming day, and Candler went back by himself into the dugout. He was content enough to be alone. There had been a time when he might have been considered gregarious, but that was a long while back.

He pulled his warbag out from under his bunk and set his spare clothes and a cloth-wrapped bundle aside. Beneath them lay the very few possessions that were important to him. He took out a small, leather-bound box with a tarnished brass latch and hinges.

There was a watch there, the key dangling from it tied by a length of thread. Candler had no idea if the watch still ran. He hadn't wound it in a very long time.

There was also a small leather folio, the leather dried with age, of the sort that was used to keep tintype photographs. He did not open it to look at the image within. He had no need to, for it was burned into memory plain enough that he could see it with his mind's eye whenever he wished. And often, too often, when he did not wish as well.

Candler did look at the folio, though, and felt a momentary pang of . . . regret? Not exactly. Not any longer. He'd gotten past regret, he believed. Wistfulness then. Perhaps that more closely called it.

He frowned, unhappy with himself for giving in to actively thinking about the past. It was something he really did not like to do.

With a scowl, he dropped the quarter eagle into the box and closed the lid, then very carefully tucked the box back into the bottom of his well-traveled and much used warbag. He picked up the tightly wrapped bundle that lay on the bed with his clothing and hefted it in his hand for a moment, then shook his head and scowled again, impatient with himself.

He kicked his boots off and walked barefoot out into the cool of the morning. A cold bath probably was just what was needed about now. And while he was in there he could get his laundry done at the same time.

Now that was efficient.

✦ 43 ✦

NORM WAS ANGRY when they returned. He was mad because he'd had to come back with the wagon, before he'd had time to drink and whore his whole pay away. Next time, he swore, he would remember and ride a damn horse in so he could come back when he wished and not when that prissy damn boss lady said they would return. Why, it was still daylight. Not even close to getting dark.

Candler listened to the big man's rantings but didn't worry about them. Norm was just peeved, that was all. He wasn't the sort of mad that could get anybody actually hurt.

And as angry as Norm was, Eddie was just the opposite. He walked around looking like a cat with little yellow feathers in the corners of its mouth.

"Looks like you had yourself a good day," Candler said to the dapper little fellow.

"Oh, yes. Very satisfying. I took Catherine and the boys to the café again." He patted his belly. "We had pork chops and fried taters and dried apple pie. Very satisfying indeed."

"Why is it that I get the idea you aren't talking just about the pork chops when you say that?" Candler said.

Eddie only laughed. And looked pleased with himself.

That evening at supper Eddie hung back when the meal was ended and Donny was starting to clear the table.

The custom was for the hired hands to leave then. It was the decent thing to do, for this was, after all, the family's private home not some boardinghouse where strangers could be expected to take their ease. The hands were welcome to eat in the house. That was only proper since there was no separate cookhouse provided for them. But once the meal was over, they were expected to go back to the dugout or sit outside to take the evening air and do their end-of-day relaxing.

This time Eddie stayed behind with another cup of coffee in his hand, his chair tipped back, acting like he had no intention of moving again for a while.

And he didn't. When Candler and Norm mumbled their thanks and grabbed for their hats, Eddie sat right where he was.

The man returned to the dugout the better part of an hour later. And this time he was as peeved as Norm Shear had been earlier in the afternoon.

Eddie yanked his clothes off like he was mad at them

and threw his hat at the wall and walked around stiff-legged and red-faced.

Candler took a look at him and rolled over so his back was toward Eddie, pretending to be asleep. Which Norm already was.

Whatever happened over there at the house after the other hands left, it had put Eddie into one foul humor now.

Not that it was any of Candler's business. Not hardly.

He closed his eyes and pushed the matter out of mind. Tomorrow would be a long day. But then weren't they all.

YOU'D HAVE THOUGHT they were about to set off on a six-months-long trail drive. Or an expedition into Darkest Africa or something. Mrs. Wolbrough's eldest chick was going to be outside the nest for the first time in his life, and the woman was clucking and fussing like an old hen.

She reminded him a good hundred times that he was to wash every meal before he ate and to wash his teeth every night and again each morning, and he shouldn't drink any of that coffee for she'd heard about cowboy coffee and it would surely stunt his growth, but he could have some of the yarb tea that she'd prepared for him and remember the tea was right there in the tin, he remembered which tin she meant didn't he, and . . .

And a thousand things more along that same line of worrying.

Poor Donny looked like he was torn between mortification at the way his mama was acting and excitement because he was going to be riding out with the grown-up hands to do a man's work and gather in the cow critters.

He was especially embarrassed when well after the break of day his mother wet the corner of her apron with a bit of spit and scrubbed a smudge off Donny's cheek, then kissed and hugged him and began to cry.

Had things been up to Candler and Eddie alone, they would have been riding out as soon as breakfast was over and the sun not yet reaching the horizon, but this morning Mrs. Wolbrough's last-moment preparations dragged on. And on. And on. The truth of it was that she just didn't want to let her baby go off by himself. Yet she looked proud of him too, knowing that he was able.

Candler suspected this was a normal enough thing with mothers and their sons and not a bad thing at all. But perhaps a mite aggravating for the boy who was having to endure it.

Eventually there wasn't anything Mrs. Wolbrough could think of rechecking or repacking, and Candler gathered up the lead for the two—count 'em, two, even though one would have been more than enough—pack horses, and the three of them mounted.

"Don't you worry about a thing, Cath . . . uh, ma'am," Eddie assured her. "I'll keep an eye on the lad. Besides,

Donny has the makings of a cowman in him. He will be just fine."

Mrs. Wolbrough barely glanced in Eddie's direction. Her attention was fully on Donny. Yesterday when they drove off to church and again last evening after their return, she had been full of chatter and cheerfulness with Eddie. Now she seemed put out with him.

For his part, Eddie seemed to have gotten over his fury of last night, but he was unusually subdued.

Candler kind of wished he'd been a fly on the wall over there in the house after supper last night.

Not that it was any of his business. No sir, it was not, and he wasn't fixing to butt his nose into any of it either. All he had to do was his job. That and draw his pay. That was the start and the end of it. Nothing more.

"You ready, son?" Eddie asked.

"Yes, sir, I sure am." Donny was grinning ear to ear, and likely would have been on the way before taking time to eat or pack anything if it had been left up to him.

"Then let's head 'em out," Eddie said. Although exactly what it was that he intended to head out Candler was not sure. There were just the three of them and the two pack animals.

But there would be more coming back than were going out, and the experience should be good for the boy regardless.

"Ma'am." Candler nodded and touched the brim of his hat, then followed along behind with the led horses while Eddie Mannet and Donny rode out.

✢ 45 ✢

I**T WAS FAR** easier going without having to make allowances for the dang wagon this time, and they could have—indeed, they should have—covered that many more miles finding a place to headquarter while they looked for Ladder cows.

Instead Eddie insisted on going back to the same camp they used before. And around which they'd already made a pretty thorough gather. In order to accomplish anything down here this time, they still would have to leave camp early and spend several hours just getting to territory they hadn't already covered.

Eddie's argument was that they already had a holding pen built at this spot, and there was water enough here too, so it would be foolish to waste time trying to find another spot as well situated. Besides, he said, with the holding pen to keep the cattle in, Donny would be free to help with the gather instead of having to keep the found cows in a bunch, three riders being that much more useful than just two.

It was an argument, Candler supposed. Never mind that he disagreed with it. And no one was asking him anyway. He unloaded the pack horses, hobbled them and turned them loose to graze on what was left of the grass after being used fairly hard that last trip.

As Candler expected, Eddie and the boy were thick, the kid following his hero around like a puppy dog at its master's heels. Candler really expected Eddie to show off his marksmanship a good bit of the time, but that did not happen.

He worked on his fast draw plenty, basking in Donny's admiration when he did so. But this time he did no practice shooting. Candler suspected Eddie's poker winnings were running dry and he could not afford more ammunition to waste shooting wood chips and songbirds.

That was all right as far as it went. The peace and quiet were certainly welcome. But if Eddie quit setting the family up to treats, Candler was going to miss having his real coffee in the mornings. He would just have to buy some himself, he supposed, if Eddie was no longer able to. The razor could wait a little while longer.

For a change Eddie Mannet was busy and productive, acting like he wanted to get this sweep finished and get back to the Ladder quickly this time.

He spent the first morning finding another hindquarter

of his version of range venison, which Candler again sank into the cool water to preserve, then concentrated on making sweeps to find and bring in strayed Ladder cows.

They were finding a good many cattle, but few of them wore the Ladder brand. Candler thought they could well be finding few because there were few left to find.

A man seldom has the wherewithal to start into the cow business on a grand scale. He takes what he has and makes do with that, starting small and depending on natural increase to let his herd grow, living off the steers and looking to his heifer calves for his family's future.

Wolbrough's spread had been like that. And now his widow apparently had no real idea how many cows she owned.

Somewhere in the house or maybe in the bank in town there would be the ledgers and tally books to fill out the picture, and if Candler had had any say in things he would have wanted to look at those before they wasted time searching for cattle that might not even exist. Why, if the books were properly kept, they might even let Mrs. Wolbrough sell her herd at book count and be back east before the first snow fell.

But John Candler was only a hired hand and knew his place, which was to knuckle his forelock and bob his head when the lady of the manor spoke. Although it did grieve him some that she seemed to know so little about the business that had supported her and her sons up to this point.

And they still were finding a Ladder hiding in the brush

every now and then, and the recovery of one good steer would pay his and Eddie's wages for the entire time they spent down here looking.

Once he thought about it that way, he was less concerned with the idea of being here.

IT WAS A banner day. Among them they'd located four Ladders. Well, four if you wanted to count the calf too. Two cows, a steer and a weanling calf that would have to be branded.

With so few likely to be discovered down here this time, Candler figured they could as easily brand any calves on the spot instead of waiting to work a bunch of them all at once.

They hadn't brought an iron with them, but the Ladder was an easy mark to make, having only the five straight lines to complete it. The burn could be put on with a cinch ring laid onto some coals and held in a piece of green wood with the end split. Candler had used that method a time or two in the past. And cow thieves did it all the time, the dual advantages being that they could duplicate almost any brand . . . and that there was nothing incriminating to be found in their gear in the event someone got to looking.

They turned the day's gather into the holding pen, and Donny closed off the entrance by dragging a pair of downed saplings into the gap. With the branches left on, they stuck up off the ground high enough to act as a barrier, although repeatedly scrubbing them over the hard ground was making them sag and go kind of limp. Candler thought they might want to cut some replacements if they were going to be down here very long this trip.

While Eddie and the boy were taking care of the cows, Candler broke up some dry wood and built the fire off what was left of the morning's coals. Covered with a layer of ash, those lasted pretty well as long as there was no rain to interfere with things. By the time the other two came in, he had the fire going and a pot of coffee water heating.

Before they left that morning, he'd dumped some dried beans into a pot of water so those could soak all day. Now the skins were wrinkled and the beans were starting to go soft; they were ready to cook. Coffee, beans and a slab of fire-seared fresh meat—it couldn't get much better.

"Bring a piece of that, uh, venison would you please, Donny?"

The boy was sitting beside Eddie. He gave Candler a dirty look. "Get it yourself if you want it."

Candler smiled sweetly. "No problem." He waded into the trickle of water that ran beside the flat and fetched out the beef. He used his belt knife to cut one steak and returned the rest to the makeshift cooler.

He dug the point of the knife into the lard can and brought out a dollop of salted lard and scraped that into the big cast-iron spider. He set that over the fire, and once the lard was melted, he plopped the steak in with a sizzle and a mouthwatering aroma.

"How come there's only one steak?"

Candler's expression never changed. "That's because I only wanted one. I'm not hungry enough to have two."

"But . . ."

"You want one, boy, go cut it yourself."

"I don't have a knife."

"Pity," Candler said, using the tip of his to move the meat around in the skillet so it wouldn't stick to the hot metal.

"Eddie? Make him cut me a steak."

Candler looked up, his expression still neutral, his eyes locked now on Eddie's. He stayed like that, hunkered down beside the fire and motionless, until Mannet cleared his throat and stood, dusting off his britches and nudging the boy.

"C'mon. I'll show you how to cut a steak proper. And cook it after."

"Eddie?"

"Come along, I said. It ain't worth arguing over."

Donny looked disappointed, but he stood and trailed along behind his hero so they could go get another pair of steaks.

✦ 47 ✦

T HE HARDEST PART of this whole deal, Candler thought, was getting the dang cinch ring into the split in the end of the stick without burning yourself. The temptation was always there to grab hold of the thing and push it in. Of course the metal ring was near to being red hot, and human skin burns even easier and quicker than cowhide does. Taking a hot cinch ring in your hand was not the sort of thing a fellow was apt to do twice. And Candler'd had his one lapse into forgetfulness already, a long time back.

He stood the ring upright against a rock, poised the open end of the stick over it and pushed.

The cinch ring fell over on its side.

"Are you soon coming with that damn iron? I can't hold this calf down forever, y'know." Eddie and the boy had dragged the calf out of the holding pen and over to the fire, where Candler was using the rings off his own saddle for the makeshift running irons.

With a sigh and a show of patience that he did not really feel, Candler used the tip of the stick to prop the ring up again, then positioned a second rock in the coals to brace the ring a little better and tried again.

He gave a grunt of satisfaction when this time the ends of the stick spread open in response to the pressure and slipped down over the glowing hot ring.

"All right, I got it. Hold him down."

He carried the ring over and had heat enough to make the first three lines, the verticals, before he had to go back to exchange that already cooling metal for the other ring lying still on the coals.

"Hold him there. I'll be right back."

Candler was bending over the fire, trying to coax the other ring into place, when he was interrupted by the sound of approaching horses. Three riders came down out of the aspens and spread out a little as they came close to the fire.

"Howdy," Candler said. "Step down and have a cup o' coffee if you'd like. You're welcome to."

None of the men showed any inclination to dismount. Two of them held saddle carbines laid across their cantles, and the third wore a pistol stuffed behind the belt of his chaps. They did not look friendly.

"That don't look like a CT brand you're putting on there," the one with the pistol said.

"No, it isn't," Candler agreed. "That's because it's a Ladder calf."

"Looks like a CT to me, mister."

"I can't help what it looks like. I only know what it is. And the cow this calf is nursing from carries a Ladder."

"You're gonna have to prove that," the CT rider said.

"Easy enough done," Candler agreed. "But we aren't gonna stress this little guy more than once. He's already been cut and earmarked and now half branded. I intend to finish what we're doing here, friend. Then we'll turn the calf in with the others in that pen over yonder. You can see then for yourself what brand is on the cow he sucks."

One of the riders wheeled his horse and rode up the slope to the holding pen. He looked inside it for a bit, then came back. By that time Candler had solved the puzzle of the awkward dang cinch ring and was applying the final two lines to form the Three I brand on the calf's flank.

"They're all Ladders in the pen, Jess. No CTs among 'em."

"That's as it may be, but we haven't seen this calf critter go suck none of them Ladders yet."

Candler nodded to Eddie and the boy. Both had been watchful throughout. But silent. That surprised Candler. He would have thought Eddie Mannet would have been sputtering and blustering. Instead he quietly continued to kneel on the calf to hold it so Candler could apply the brand.

"Let him up now, please."

Eddie stood. Donny was a little slow to move, but the

calf wasn't. It came up with a lurch and a bawl, knocking the boy backward while the calf switched its tail angrily and ran to the pen and its mama.

"Go pull that pole aside so the calf can get in, Donny," Candler instructed.

This time the boy gave him no argument but ran to do as he was told.

The three CT men rode over and watched as the calf ran for the comfort of its mother's side and immediately began to butt her bag and noisily suck while the lophorned old cow licked the fresh burns on her baby's hide.

"The calf is a Ladder all right," the leader of the CTs said. "No offense intended, you understand."

"None taken," Candler agreed. "You've a right to ask."

"All right then."

"The offer of coffee is still open."

The CT man glanced toward Eddie, who looked like he was building up a head of steam now that things were calm and agreeable. "No, we'd best get along. Thanks for the invite though."

"Any time," Candler said. "Stop by any time you like."

The CT man touched the brim of his hat and reined away, the two with the rifles turning to follow.

They politely held their horses to a walk until they were well clear of the camp area, then bumped the animals into a lope.

"Cheeky bastards," Eddie said.

Candler did not bother to reply. He went back to the fire to reclaim his cinch rings. As soon as they were cool, he needed to clean the burnt hair off of them and put them back onto his cinch where they belonged.

✥ 48 ✥

THEY DIDN'T DO all that much good. Eighteen head after two weeks of looking, and after two weeks even Eddie Mannet had to admit that they were wasting their time. They hadn't found a Ladder animal in four days and no longer had much hope of gathering more.

"We'll start home tomorrow morning," he announced. "Meantime I'm gonna go find us some more venison. We're out."

"It'd just be that much more to pack," Candler reminded him. "And I saw Jess and one of those other CT boys this afternoon. I think they're looking us over again."

Eddie frowned. But he said nothing more about going out to look for range venison, it very likely having been CT beef that they were eating this whole time. Killing another CT beef would be sure to rile those riders.

If any of them were in the neighborhood. Candler had seen no such thing that afternoon. He just didn't want Eddie wasting another of someone else's property so the three of them could get one meal out of it.

"We have plenty enough cornmeal left and a little lard," he said. "I'll cook us up a good feed and make enough to have cold tomorrow morning too. That'll let us get an early start and maybe we can get these critters back in one day's time." He smiled. "Sleep in a proper bed for a change tomorrow night."

"I've had fun," Donny said.

"But you won't mind sleeping in your own bed tomorrow night? An' having some of your mama's cooking instead of mine?"

The kid grinned. "I could stand it."

"Yeah, well, we're glad you've had a good time. Been a good help too. You have a nose for where to find 'em, and you're learning how to work those cows just fine."

"D'you really think so?" The boy looked pleased.

"Of course he thinks so," Eddie said. "We both do."

Donny hadn't clung quite so close to Eddie after the CT riders came by. Candler understood why, of course. Eddie had based the boy's opinion of him on his ability to get a gun quickly out of a holster. When Jess and the others rode in, Donny expected Eddie to challenge them and did not understand when Eddie prudently kept his mouth shut. They were in the right, after all, and there was no need to turn it into a fight.

The yonker did not yet understand that when little boys

fight, a bloodied nose and some hurt feelings are about the worst that can happen. When grown men get into it, someone can end up buried.

That was all right. He had time enough to learn about such things.

"Donny, why don't you make the coffee tonight while I put the dough together."

"Me? You want me to make the coffee?"

"You've seen it done often enough, and it isn't like it's difficult. You can do it as good as either of us can."

The boy grinned and grabbed up the pan Candler always used to make the coffee in, running down to the creek to rinse it out and fill it.

✦ 49 ✦

I T WAS PAST dark by the time they got back to the Ladder, but none of them seemed to mind pushing those
last few miles to reach the comforts of home. Well, such as
it was.

For Candler, and he assumed for Eddie too, however
temporary the job, right here and right now this was home.
Or as close to one as either of them was likely to come.

To Donny it really was home, and he seemed eager to
see his mama again. Maybe even didn't mind the thought
of seeing his baby brother. Candler supposed all baby
brothers were mostly annoying, but also loved, although a
kid Donny's age would not likely admit to that.

Regardless of the reasons, Donny seemed the most
pleased of them all when they reached the Ladder and
turned the cows into the horse trap rather than have them

go looking for the main herd in the dark. They were as apt to spook the cattle as add to them if they went blundering around in the middle of the night.

Norm was in the dugout. He'd had his supper and was grabbing a little sleep before he went out to ride nightherd.

"I'm glad to see youse guys back," he told them. "I ain't been sleeping much while you been gone, watching over them most of the day and most of the night too and catching some sack time here an' there. Now maybe I can get some proper sleep again."

"Maybe we all can," Candler agreed.

"You want I should take those new cows out and put 'em with the others?"

"That would be a big help, Norm, thanks."

Donny had run on ahead to the house as soon as the horses were unsaddled and turned into the corral. Lights were showing at the window and door now and pretty soon Donny came trotting down to the dugout.

"Mama says she'll have some supper for us quick as a flash."

"We'll be up to get it soon as we dump our stuff and wash up," Candler told him.

Eddie remained silent throughout the homecoming, even when a woman-cooked supper was mentioned. Feeling off his feed, Candler thought. Maybe had a bellyache or like that.

"Tell your mama we won't be long."

"All right, but if you aren't there when it hits the table, she'll throw it to the pigs."

Candler smiled. There might be some pigs somewhere in the county, but damned if he'd know where. Certainly there were none on the Ladder. "We'll be right along."

He walked over to the horse trap and handled the gate while Norm rode in and put the cows into a bunch then moved them out.

Norm was good with cattle. He wasn't the smartest fellow Candler had ever met, but he was honest and a good worker and he could work cows about as well as anybody Candler ever met. He never hurried them. That was something Candler had noticed about the way Norm moved cattle around. He got what he wanted across to them without getting them riled up or nervous, and he never tried to rush them into doing it.

Candler let Norm and the cows get clear, then closed the gate again and walked back down to the dugout. It was empty, so apparently Eddie and the boy had already gone over to the house. Candler change into a slightly less dirty shirt and paused outside to scrape some of the dried cow shit off his boots, then hurried to join the others.

It would be a shame to let Mrs. Wolbrough's good cooking get thrown to the pigs.

✦ 50 ✦

"WE SHALL GO to town tomorrow," Mrs. Wolbrough announced at supper a couple days later. "It is my understanding you have gathered as many of the Three I cattle as are likely to be found. Is that correct, Mr. Mannet?"

Eddie nodded. He did not look happy about the admission, but he was pretty well forced to make it.

"Very well. We shall drive to town tomorrow, and I shall purchase supplies for a trip down to the railroad. That is . . . how far would you say?"

Eddie shook his head. "I don't know."

"Mr. Chandler?"

"About a hundred twenty miles, ma'am. Give or take a little."

"And the cattle can travel how fast?"

"That depends on what condition you want them to be

in when they get there. We could push them hard and have them there in a week, but they'd be in better flesh and worth more to the buyers if we plan on it being more like two weeks on the way."

"You really intend to sell them then?" Eddie asked.

"Of course. Just as I have all along. Just as I told you last night."

Candler wondered just what that little exchange was about. Eddie suggested she not sell her cows? He wondered what reason he could possibly have offered for that. And for that matter wondered why Eddie would care. They weren't his cattle, after all.

"I think you are making a mistake, Catherine."

"I will thank you to address me properly, Mr. Mannet. We are employer and employee. Please bear that in mind."

Eddie looked like there ought to be steam spurting out his ears. Otherwise the pressure inside him was apt to overload his skull, and he'd blow up like an overloaded boiler tank.

Norm reached for the bowl of rice and the gravy boat, oblivious to the whole thing. Donny looked curious. And Candler, if the truth be known, was fascinated.

He was beginning to understand, though. Thought he did anyway. And it made sense, down to and including Eddie insisting that they make those sweeps around the perimeter of the Ladder.

For weeks now Eddie had been planning to take over the Ladder and run it himself. Probably suggested some cockamamie scheme for him to act as ranch manager while

Mrs. Wolbrough and the boys went on back east. He would market the increase and the culls every year, keep out his own wage and send the rest east.

Sure. Except of course on a little place like the Ladder there wouldn't be enough profit to make that worthwhile. It would be just fine for Eddie Mannet but not much point in it for Mrs. Wolbrough and her sons.

Eddie did have cheek. Candler had to give him credit for that.

"I will pay each of you another two dollars," Mrs. Wolbrough said, obviously closing the subject of Eddie Mannet's plans for her cattle. "You can take tomorrow and the next day off. The morning after that we shall start south. All of us. I will drive the wagon and keep James with me."

"You don't have to come," Eddie said. "I can—"

"No!" Her voice was sharp, offering no room for argument. "I am perfectly capable of arranging the sale myself, thank you. They are, after all, my cattle. I shall undertake the negotiation without your . . . assistance."

Candler was not at all sure that "assistance" would have been her first choice of words there. "Interference" might have applied as easily. But she did not say that. Quite.

"Are there any other questions?"

"No, ma'am," Candler said. "We'll be ready. That's no problem."

"No." Eddie's voice was just short of insolence.

"Can I have another of them corn dodgers please, ma'am?"

Candler hid a smile. Good-hearted Norm. Feed him and let him whoop it up every once in a while—that was all he asked. Mrs. Wolbrough passed him the platter of corn muffins.

✦ 51 ✦

A MAN COULD get pretty drunk on two dollars. Eddie Mannet proved it. Quick as they hit town, he was in the nearest saloon pouring down a beer and a shot, and he kept them coming. No cards for him this trip. No women. He just wanted to drink until he was out or the money was, whichever one of those came first. Candler wasn't sure, but he thought it would pretty much work out to a tie.

He and Norm stayed with Mrs. Wolbrough long enough to help her load the provisions she'd bought for the road trip. And to offer a few suggestions as to what should be included. Then Mrs. Wolbrough took her boys and went off visiting friends.

"We shall be leaving at sundown, Mr. Chandler. Please see that all of you are ready at that time."

"Yes, ma'am."

Norm bought a pocketful of candies for the journey—
Candler doubted they would last until the start of the trip,
never mind the end of it—and then the two of them joined
Eddie in the saloon.

It was a funny thing about that. Candler did not like Eddie Mannet. He was not the sort Candler liked to be
around. And he liked Norm well enough but had few interests in common that they might talk about, Norm's span of
interest being limited to food, cows and sleep. But they
were a crew. In that respect they were one entity and they
stuck together, lined up along the bar.

Eddie stayed there all day long, his voice getting thicker
and his legs weaker as the day wore on. Norm had some
beer. Went to buy a lunch. Came back for beer, left again
with a woman and returned finally to concentrate on the
beer. Candler, well, Candler had a relaxing time of it too,
more along the lines of Norm's day than Eddie's.

Close to sundown Candler got the wagon and brought it
around so they could load Eddie into it. Norm simply
picked Eddie up, easy as if he were a scarecrow stuffed
with a little straw, instead of a grown man, and deposited
him into the wagon along with the sacks and the boxes that
would feed the six of them for the next couple weeks. Then
they went to find Mrs. Wolbrough and the boys so they
could go back to the Ladder.

It occurred to Candler that he did not think in terms of going "home" again now. The Ladder's dugout had been home
for a little while there, but no longer. Home once again now
was wherever he happened to drop his saddle and warbag.

They drove back with Candler handling the lines, the boys chattering to their mama, Norm whistling a tune Candler could not identify and Eddie in the back snoring.

All in all, he thought, a thoroughly relaxing day.

✦ 52 ✦

"BISH," EDDIE DECLARED rather loudly. They had deposited him on his bunk but he was waking up now. Norm was already in bed sound asleep, and Candler hoped to be that way himself in another minute or two.

"Bish," Eddie repeated, louder this time.

Candler ignored him. He was busy folding and arranging everything in his warbag. They would in all likelihood be paid off at the railhead and, once they rode out, would not be returning to the Ladder again. Mrs. Wolbrough would not likely need their help to sell the horses and do her packing so she and the boys could take their leave too.

Eddie sat up and scratched himself. It said something about his powers of recuperation that he could do that. He had been pretty well soaked when they left town. Now he just looked angry. Drunk too. But to outward appearances mostly angry.

"She is, y'know."

Candler tried to pay him no mind.

"Are you lis'nin' to me? You know what I'm talkin' 'bout here?"

"Of course I do," Candler lied. He didn't know. Didn't care about a drunk's ramblings either.

"She's a bish . . ." Eddie shook his head. "Bitch," he corrected himself. "What d'you say t' that, huh?"

"Oh, I wouldn't know anything about it."

"Well, I would. Damn her. Bitch." Eddie ran his hands over his head, smoothing down his hair and looking like he was trying to smooth down his face as well. Could be it felt like it was in danger of falling off. "Bitch."

"Uh huh."

"Thinks she's s' damn good. Too good for the likes o' me. Tha's wha' she thinks. Bitch."

"Uh huh."

"Offered t' marry her, damn her. Did, y'know. Woulda married her. In that stinkin' church o' hers. I woulda."

"Uh huh." But of course he had not known. And would have thought the idea ludicrous if he had known about Eddie's proposal. Catherine Wolbrough and a would-be sharpie like Eddie? Candler never met the late Mr. Wolbrough, but he doubted the man had been much like Eddie. Whatever he was like he had been man enough to make an eastern lady satisfied with a ranch wife's life for as long as he was alive, and that was something right there. Not much like Eddie at all, Candler suspected.

"Bish . . . bitch . . . too good to marry with me, down an' out widda woman like that . . . oughta be pl . . . plea . . . oughta be happy a man'd look at her . . . an' her with two shitty brats hanging on her . . . bitch."

"Uh huh." Candler revised his earlier suspicion. Eddie hadn't wanted to be the Ladder's manager. The idiot wanted to be its owner. Marry the widow and take possession of the Ladder with its improvements, its grass and water, its cows to use and grow on them. That was his plan, not just being a caretaker on someone else's ground. He wanted to own it himself.

Not that Candler could blame Eddie for dreaming about improving his situation. Candler had had dreams of his own once.

"I'll fix her, though," Eddie declared. "You'll see. I'll fix that bitch, I will."

"Uh huh. Sure you will."

Candler finished his folding and fussing. He closed the warbag and slid it beneath the bed he'd built when they first got here. That bag, his bedroll and the saddle rigging that was draped over a fence rail outside were all he owned and all he had to worry about. He was ready now to move along to whatever else he could find. It did not matter where and it did not much matter what. He would get along.

Eddie was still muttering when Candler blew out the lamp and turned in for the night.

✦ 53 ✦

THERE WAS NO sign of Eddie Mannet when Candler woke up the next morning. He bunk was empty. Eddie's trunk was there, but his bedroll was gone. Candler wondered if he'd gotten so worked up about Mrs. Wolbrough spurning his proposal of marriage that Eddie decided to pull out now and leave just the two men and Donny to take the cows down to the railroad. Except the trunk was there. Eddie surely would not leave that behind.

Candler pulled his britches on and stepped into his boots. He stretched and rubbed his chin, thinking he really did need to buy a razor of his own. Should have gotten one when they were in town yesterday. He kept forgetting to do that, darn it.

"Norm? Time for breakfast, Norm." That would bring Shear awake. The prospect of a meal would rouse him anytime, and Norm hadn't been drunk last night. A little mellow perhaps but not what Candler would call drunk. Not like Eddie had been.

"I'm coming," Norm mumbled. "Be right there."

Candler went outside, enjoying the invigorating chill in the predawn air. He stretched again and rotated his shoulders. He felt pretty good everything considered. He used the outhouse and stretched once again when he stepped back outside.

Across the way the house was showing light, and there was a lantern sitting on a stool beside the front door. Candler poured water into the washbasin, the water cold from sitting out overnight, and hung his hat on a peg driven into the wall close by for that purpose.

He took a double handful of the cold water and dunked his face in it. Now that would wake a man up right quick. He shivered and groaned a little. But he liked the feel of freshness once the shock of the cold was ended.

When he was finished washing up, he went around to the front and tapped lightly on the door before opening it and stepping inside.

There was no sign of Mrs. Wolbrough and no fire in the range. No food cooking. No coffee at the boil. Candler frowned. What the hell was going on here?

"Mr. Chandler." Her voice came from behind him, came from outside. She'd been out there in the dark somewhere but he hadn't seen her. "Have you seen Donald, Mr. Chandler?"

"Ma'am?"

"I cannot find Donald. He isn't in his bed, and I can't find him anywhere outside either. Do you happen to know where he is?"

"No, ma'am."

Eddie was gone. And now so was Donny?

What sort of crazy game was Eddie playing here? Candler wondered. For with the two of them missing, it was certainly Eddie's doing. Another of Eddie's plans.

Except why would he take the boy with him? It would do no good just to delay Mrs. Wolbrough taking her cattle down to the railroad. No matter when she took them they still were hers to take. Delay would not change that simple fact.

Candler felt a chill that had nothing to do with the cool of the weather or the cold of the water he'd washed with.

If Eddie wanted to scare the woman, this was probably one hell of a good way to do it. But surely he did not think he could frighten her into a marriage. Blackmail then? Force her to sign over her rights to the land?

Hell, he wouldn't have to kidnap Donny to accomplish that. Probably she would have been willing to relinquish her right to the land just for the asking. If the place hadn't been proven up on, then there was no value to the claim anyway. And no value to the land rights without cows to use the grass. Surely Eddie could see that.

The truth was, though, that Candler had no idea what Eddie Mannet could see or couldn't. So far his planning had been unrealistic but harmless.

This could turn out to be something else. Something a whole lot more serious.

"We'll look for him, ma'am."

Norm was on his way over to the house, expecting breakfast. Candler intercepted him. "Come on, Norm. We have to look around. See if we can find Eddie and Donny."

"Where'd they go?"

"That's what you and I have to find out."

"What about somethin' to eat, huh?"

"Later, Norm."

The big man sighed but he was agreeable. He turned around and headed toward the corral, which would be the obvious place to start. If their saddles were gone—and they probably were—it would mean the two could be almost anywhere.

Candler hoped Donny was in no physical danger from Eddie, then was upset with himself for even thinking such a thing. Eddie was unrealistic but surely he wasn't that crazy.

Or was he?

Unconsciously Candler increased his pace until he was almost running toward the corral.

✢ 54 ✢

THREE HORSES WERE missing, the two Eddie and Donny favored and the horse Candler had used as their pack animal on that swing down south. Whatever this was about, they expected to be gone for a spell.

"They ain't gonna try and take the cows by themselves just the two of 'em, are they?" Norm asked.

"No, I wouldn't think so. I can't see there would be any point to that."

"You want I should go hold the cows bunched then?" Norm asked.

"That's probably a good idea, Norm."

"Can I eat breakfast first?"

"We aren't having breakfast this morning, I don't think."

"No breakfast?"

"Mrs. Wolbough is upset about not being able to find Donny," Candler explained.

"Lunch then?"

"Sure. Come in then. I'll see that there's a lunch for you."

Norm smiled. "Thanks." He took the rope down off his saddle on the top rail and slipped inside the corral to catch his horse and get ready for an ordinary day of work, unconcerned about the things that worried others.

Candler went back to the house to tell Mrs. Wolbrough. He needn't have bothered. She already knew.

The lady was in her kitchen. The little guy James was seated at the table in the place Norm usually occupied. There still was no fire built in the range.

"James tells me that Mr. Mannet came up the ladder to wake Donald some time during the night. James overheard them whispering. Mr. Mannet told Donald to dress for the trail. He said they had a job to do but James doesn't remember if he said what the job was."

Not that it mattered, Candler thought. Whatever Eddie said would have been a lie intended to get Donny away as a voluntary participant in his own kidnapping.

"He said something about going somewhere far away." The woman was trying not to cry, but she was not being very successful at the effort. "I know why he did this," she said. "He wants . . . There is something he wants me to do. Something he tried . . . tried to force me to do."

So it wasn't just the cows, Candler thought. Eddie wanted a woman he could use too. Although Candler sus-

pected that would just be a bonus. The cows, the ranch—
those were what probably mattered the most.

Candler did not let on that he knew what Mrs. Wolbrough was talking about.

"He left a note," she said. "He slipped it under Donald's
pillow. Can you read, Mr. Chandler?"

"Yes, ma'am, I can read," Candler said without elabora-
tion.

She dug into the pocket of her apron and produced a
scrap of butcher paper with barely legible pencil markings
on it: "you wont find him wont see him agin til you know
what ill get answer later you think bout it here ill be back
you dont know when dont look ill fine you stay here"

Candler read it twice, canting the paper to one side to
catch the light so he could make out the words. Then he
handed it back without comment.

"I need for you to go to town for me today, Mr. Chandler."

"Yes, ma'am?"

"I shall write a letter to the county sheriff. I of course
intend to have Mr. Mannet prosecuted to the fullest extent
of the law."

"You know how long a letter will take to reach the sheriff, ma'am? It'll be days at the least. And then he may not
do much about it. You just told me yourself that Donny got
up and went along with Eddie. He wasn't forced to go.
Might've been lied to, but he wasn't forced."

"Even so . . ."

"Yes, ma'am. You are calling in the law. Such as it is.
I'm sure that's the best thing for you to do."

"You do not sound as if you share that opinion, Mr. Chandler."

"No, ma'am, but it isn't my decision to make." There had been a time when Candler made decisions. For himself and for a good many other men as well. He turned his back on all of that years ago. Now he just went along. Did what he was told. Thought about very little.

Most of the time.

"I'll go get saddled, ma'am. You write your letter."

"Thank you, Mr. Chandler."

"Oh, and ma'am?"

"Yes?"

"It's Norm, ma'am. He'll be back in for lunch after a bit. It'd be nice if there was something for him to eat when he gets here. Norm sets store by his food times, ma'am. It's important to him."

"Yes, I'll . . . I will do that, thank you."

Candler touched the brim of his hat and turned for the door. "I'll fetch a horse and be right back, ma'am. You have that letter ready. I'll see it gets mailed."

He stepped back outside. A pink, rose and golden glow was spreading into the sky to the east, the first rays of the as yet unseen sun lighting up a scattering of high cloud. The day promised to be a beautiful one.

CANDLER WAS ALREADY packed, so he did not have to take time to do that, but he did fetch out the little box that held his treasures and take the quarter eagle gold coin out. He transferred it to his pants pocket and replaced everything else as it had been.

He carried his warbag out to the corral, where his saddle was, and tied the warbag and his canvas-wrapped blanket roll behind the cantle, then saddled the steeldust horse. It was his favorite among the ones he'd been given for his string.

He took his time. Mrs. Wolbrough would need a few minutes to compose her letter. To compose herself too for that matter.

Besides, there was no hurry now. Eddie and the boy had a head start of hours, perhaps most of the night, and their start would be days greater by the time the county sheriff even learned about it. And there was no guarantee he would see fit to do anything once he did find out. It could not even be said with certainty that a crime had been committed here. Not by the standards of the law anyway. So there was no sense in rushing off now.

Candler led the steeldust out and closed the corral gate behind him, then walked the horse over to the house. It was full daylight by the time he got there.

He tapped at the door frame. "I'm ready to leave whenever you have that letter, ma'am."

"Yes. I'll just be another minute."

She hurriedly finished writing, folded the paper over and looked around for an envelope to contain it. Eventually she settled for enclosing her note in another sheet of plain paper and gluing that closed, then writing "Sheriff Markham" on it.

"I don't know the address, but . . ."

"Don't worry about that, ma'am. I'll get the clerk at the postal window to put it right."

"Very well. Thank you." She handed the letter to him.

"Yes, ma'am. I'll get it off quick as I can."

"Thank you." She gave him a closer look. "You are being very helpful."

"My pleasure, ma'am."

"I never . . . Excuse me, but I suppose I never noticed before. Do you know, if it weren't for that birthmark you would be a very nice-looking man."

He laughed. "Not likely, ma'am, but it's nice of you to say so."

That wasn't something he liked to think about. But there had indeed been a time. And the disfigurement of his face was not a birthmark.

"I'll be leaving now," he said. "Get this into the mail quick as I can."

"Yes. Thank you."

Candler touched the brim of his hat and let himself out. Behind him he could hear James beginning to whine for his breakfast.

✛ 56 ✛

"Trouble out at the Three I's?" the postal clerk asked. Postal clerk now. The man was the keeper of the store where the post office cubicle was located, but when he put on his green eyeshade and stepped behind the postal window he became an official representative of the United States government. Which probably made his natural nosiness an official function as well. "We don't generally see letters going to the sheriff."

Candler only shrugged. "Miz Wolbrough asked me to mail it. She didn't tell me what was in it." Which was, technically speaking, entirely true. He had never read the wording she chose to use.

The gent's face pinched in on itself, not liking Candler's answer, but he took the letter and quickly completed the address on it. "That will be three cents."

Candler dug some change out of his pocket and paid for the stamp. "I'd like to buy a few things too while I'm here."

"At that counter then, please." The clerk used a set of rubber stamps to cancel the stamp he'd just pasted onto Mrs. Wolbrough's letter, then dropped it into a box on a shelf behind him.

"When will that go out?" Candler asked.

"Day after tomorrow."

"All right, thanks."

The clerk removed the eyeshade and hung it on a hook behind the postal cage, then adjusted his apron and sleeve garters as he once again became a storekeeper.

"Now, what is it that you will be needing today?"

Candler paused for a moment to consider. "Some coffee. The ready ground and roasted, please. Say a half pound of that. Two pound of pinto beans. Two pound of wheat flour. Half cup of lard. Quarter cup of salt. Do you have jerked beef?"

"I have dried antelope. Will that do?"

Candler did not like the dark, stringy antelope nearly as well as beef. But it would do. He nodded.

"Anything else?"

"Do you have any of the paper cartridges for cap-and-ball revolvers?"

"I still carry some of those."

"Let me have a carton of the .36-calibers then, please. And a tin of percussion caps."

"I'll have to get them from the back. I won't be but a moment."

He returned and placed a yellow pasteboard box on the counter beside Candler's other selections.

"That will be all I need then," Candler said, laying his quarter eagle coin down.

"Moving on, are you?" the clerk asked, his expression again saying louder than words that he disapproved of these itinerant cowhands who roamed here and there without any settled permanence.

"Something like that," Candler said as he gathered his change and his purchases. "Thanks for your help."

The clerk did not bother to respond. But then he was unlikely ever to see this particular cowhand again and had no further need to be friendly to him.

H<small>E TOOK THE</small> road south toward the distant railroad but late in the afternoon reined off the marked and rutted public roadway and cut across country.

He spent the night beside someone's windmill, serenaded to sleep by the creaking of the turning fan and the sucker rod and by the quiet comings and goings of the cows and other creatures that came to drink at the artificial pond that may once have been a buffalo wallow.

In the morning he took time to prepare a stout breakfast before he rubbed the steeldust down and set his saddle in place.

There was a chill in the air that suggested autumn would not be long in coming, and he spent a few moments with the bit clutched in his hand so the metal would be body temperature before he slipped it into the horse's mouth.

Then he pulled his cinches tight, stepped onto a cold leather seat—it was no dang wonder so many horsemen got the piles, he thought, not for the first time—and started out again, this time angling westward away from the road, toward the line of distant hills he could see lying low on the horizon.

He had never been this exact route before, but he thought he could find the spot he wanted. Or anyway find something close enough to it that he would recognize where he was and find his way there.

✢ 58 ✢

"HELLO, BOY," CANDLER said, bringing the steeldust to a halt a few yards downwind from the campfire, where dust from the horse's hoofs would not drift onto their food. "Mind if I step down?"

Donny shrugged. "You come down to help us? I thought me and Eddie was supposed to do on our own this time."

"Yes, I came down to help." Apparently the boy believed they were told to look for more cattle, Candler guessed. That sounded right. It was the sort of thing they'd been doing right along and something Donny would accept without question if he thought his mother—or his idol Eddie—wanted to gather a few more before they took the herd away to market.

"Where is Eddie?" Candler asked, bending to put the hobbles onto the steeldust.

"I'm here, you son of a bitch." Eddie was coming down out of the aspens with an armload of dry blowdown branches for the fire.

He was wearing his pistols, Candler saw.

"You don't look glad to see me."

"You shouldn't have come here, you freak-faced son of a bitch." Eddie dropped the firewood and hitched his trousers up.

Donny looked confused.

"The thing is," Candler said, looking at the boy, "you've been kidnapped. Bet you didn't know that, did you?"

"I don't understand."

"That's all right. Your mama will explain everything to you when you get home. I'm going to take you there now."

"The hell you say," Eddie roared.

Candler straightened and slid a hand inside the middle of his bedroll. He brought out an antiquated revolver, not an actual Colt but one of the Southern-made copies that aped the Colt design at a time when genuine arms from the Colt works in Connecticut could not be obtained.

Candler stuck the long, slender barrel of the old gun into his waistband. "You don't have anything to say about it, Eddie. You made a mistake. I can understand that. Mrs. Wolbrough has everything you've ever dreamed of, and she just wants to get shut of it so she can leave. Go back east and be a regular lady again. You want . . . you want what she has. This isn't the way to get it, Eddie. She's written to the county sheriff. There's no way you could have that land now no matter what else happens. What I'd suggest you should do is get on that horse . . . I don't think the lady will object if you keep it . . . and ride away. I doubt anybody will look for you. Not very hard anyhow. So just . . . mount up and go, Eddie."

The boy looked confused.

"Damn you, Candler, this is none of your business."

"You are probably right about that, Eddie. I didn't want to be, but I'm in it now. So light out of here while you still can. I'll see the boy gets home."

"Eddie, what is he talking about?" Donny complained. "I don't like this. What is he saying?"

"He's full of lies, son. That's all. He's just full of lies."

"Are you going to shoot him?"

"Yeah. Yeah, boy, I'm gonna shoot him." Eddie glared at Candler. "You're the one better mount up and move along, John. Or I'll shoot you down. I swear I will. You can't stand up against me. You've seen me shoot. You know how fast I am."

"I've seen you shoot," Candler agreed. "You're as fast as any man I've ever seen."

"You can't stand against that. Now get out of here."

"No, Eddie, I don't expect I can do that."

"I'll shoot, John. You know I will."

"Eddie, I've seen you shoot, but I've not seen you kill. Have you killed men before, Eddie? I have. More than I like to think about. More than I ever wanted. But I've killed. I killed the man who put these powder burns on my face. I killed him and two other damn yankee sons of bitches that were with him."

Candler killed more than those soldiers that day too. He killed his own hopes for the future when that yank shot part of his face away and left a spray of gunpowder in the wounds. His fiancée took one look at him afterward and turned her back. She never spoke to him again.

But yes. Candler knew what it was to kill. And facing another man with a gun took more than speed. It took steel.

Candler did not believe Eddie Mannet had that steel inside him. He had the bluster but not the belly. ·

"I'm here, Eddie. I'm taking the boy home now. I'd like it if you just leave now."

"You go to hell, John."

Eddie's right hand flashed and his pistol cleared leather in the space of a heartbeat.

Candler was not ruffled by the huge spray of fire and pale smoke that blossomed around the muzzle of Eddie's pistol.

He stepped sideways, out of the line of Eddie's concentration, and drew his own old revolver with deliberate speed. His hand was steady and his own aim sure.

Eddie had time to loose two shots and cock his pistol for the third before Candler fired.

But Candler needed to fire only the once.

His bullet struck Eddie Mannet in the throat.

Eddie's eyes went wide. In the shock of realization? Perhaps. No one would ever know. Eddie was dead before his knees buckled and he plunged facedown onto the hard ground beside the campfire.

Candler stood silent for a moment, saddened. Then he stuffed the old .36 out of sight again.

"Come on, boy," he said. "We have to take care of things here, then get you home. Your mama is worried about you."

Donny was staring at his dead idol. Disbelieving. Shocked. That was all right. The yonker had learned much this summer. This would be his final lesson.

Damn Eddie anyway.

Candler began getting them ready to take Eddie's body back to town for a pauper's burial. Likely they would be able to sell those pretty guns for enough to pay for that.

But first he had to get the boy home. His mother was worrying.

And then . . . He looked down at the empty husk that had been a man. . . . It had been years. But Candler wanted to go home now too.

From Spur Award-winning author
FRANK RODERUS

Winter Kill	0-425-18099-9
Dead Man's Journey	0-425-18554-0
Siege	0-425-18883-3
Judgement Day	0-425-19937-1

"Frank Roderus writes a lean, tough book."
—Douglas Hirt

"Frank Roderus makes the West seem
so real, you'd swear he'd been
there himself long ago."
—Jory Sherman

Available wherever books are sold or at
www.penguin.com

B074

Spur Award-Winning Author

Jory Sherman

Texas Dust

When Joby Redmond returned from war,
he thought he had put the killing
behind him. But when his lifelong
enemy appears—and begins terrorizing
the Redmond family—Joby knows
the fight is far from over.

0-425-19430-2

Available wherever books are sold or at
www.penguin.com

B159

EDITED BY

ROBERT J. RANDISI

WHITE HATS

BUFFALO BILL CODY, BAT MASTERSON,
AND OTHER LEGENDARY HEROIC FIGURES OF
AMERICA'S OLD WEST GET THE ROYAL
TREATMENT IN 16 STORIES FROM ESTEEMED
WESTERN AUTHORS.

0-425-18426-9

BLACK HATS

A WESTERN ANTHOLOGY THAT INCLUDES TALES
OF BUTCH CASSIDY, NED CHRISTIE, SAM BASS
AND OTHER HISTORICAL VILLAINS FROM
THE WILD WEST.

0-425-18708-X

AVAILABLE WHEREVER BOOKS ARE SOLD OR AT
WWW.PENGUIN.COM

B078

"MAKE ROOM ON YOUR SHELF OF FAVORITES
FOR PETER BRANVOLD."
—FRANK RODERUS

THE DEVIL GETS HIS DUE

A LOU PROPHET NOVEL BY

PETER BRANVOLD

On the trail with Louisa Bonaventure,
"The Vengeance Queen," bounty hunter Lou
Prophet is caught in a bloody crossfire of hatred
between an outlaw who would shoot a man dead
for fun and Louisa, who has sworn to kill him—
even if she dies trying.

"THE NEXT LOUIS L'AMOUR."
—ROSEANNE BITTNER

0-425-19454-X

AVAILABLE WHEREVER BOOKS ARE SOLD OR AT
WWW.PENGUIN.COM

B248

Penguin Group (USA) Inc. Online

What will you be reading tomorrow?

Tom Clancy, Patricia Cornwell, W.E.B. Griffin,
Nora Roberts, William Gibson, Robin Cook,
Brian Jacques, Catherine Coulter, Stephen King,
Dean Koontz, Ken Follett, Clive Cussler,
Eric Jerome Dickey, John Sandford,
Terry McMillan…

You'll find them all at
http://www.penguin.com

*Read excerpts and newsletters, find tour
schedules, and enter contest.*

Subscribe to Penguin Group (USA) Inc. Newsletters
and get an exclusive inside look
at exciting new titles and the authors you love
long before everyone else does.

PENGUIN GROUP (USA) INC. NEWS
http://www.penguin.com/news